T0149241

Somerville

Somerville

A CHRISTIAN NOVEL
RITA COKER

iUniverse

SOMERVILLE
A CHRISTIAN NOVEL

iUniverse books may be ordered through booksellers or by contacting:

iUniverse
1663 Liberty Drive
Bloomington, IN 47403
www.iuniverse.com
844-349-9409

KJV
Scripture quotations marked KJV are from the Holy Bible, King James Version (Authorized Version). First published in 1611. Quoted from the KJV Classic Reference Bible, Copyright © 1983 by "http://www.zondervan.com/" Zondervan Corporation.

ISBN: 978-1-6632-1037-1 (sc)
ISBN: 978-1-6632-1038-8 (e)

Print information available on the last page.

iUniverse rev. date: 10/07/2020

Chapter 1

It was an ordinary Sunday morning in the little town of Somerville, located in northwest Mississippi. Lights began to come on in most of the homes. No one expected that this would be the day that would change the world as they had known it. The routine was much the same for most families. Everyone got dressed for church and gathered together for breakfast. The first one in the kitchen automatically turned on the radio. Instead of the local news and the weather, they heard the announcer's voice elevated and shaking.

"We have just been informed that there has been a surprise attack at Pearl Harbor. Japanese planes came in two waves. The first was at 7:53 AM. The second hit at 8:55. Everything happened so fast and with such precision, it was over at 9:55. The planes were launched from carriers. They were on their way back to Japan by 1:00 PM."

Later the report came that about 2400 were dead. The Pacific Fleet was crippled, 188 destroyed planes and 8 damaged or destroyed battleships. Chaos and confusion dominated even the brightest minds. No one doubted that there was no longer any need for more discussions as to the Americans determining what part they should have in the

German defeat of France that left England to fight the evil Nazi terror alone.

Soon almost everyone had gathered around their radios. Frozen with fear, they sat staring at each other, some crying and others filled with rage. There was some security in knowing that Somerville was located in the central part of the United States. That security didn't last long before reality set in and they knew that when one part of our country was attacked, every American would suffer in some way.

The Christian community knew instinctively that the best thing for them was to gather at their local churches. The only thing they could do to help would be to pray for God's presence, peace and protection to surround all those men and women in harm's way. Everyone must pray diligently for their President asking God to give him wisdom, understanding and courage for this horrendous trial. As the prayer warriors approached the throne room of God in their spirits, they kept a radio playing so that they could stay informed. The next news they heard made them know that God was answering their prayers for their President.

In Washington, D.C., President Franklin D. Roosevelt received a call from Winston Churchill telling him that the Japanese had attacked British colonies in Southeast Asia and that Britain would declare war immediately. Roosevelt told Churchill that he would go before Congress the next day and ask for a declaration of war against Japan. Churchill wrote: "To have the United States at our side was to me the greatest joy. Now at this very moment I knew the United States was in the war, up to the neck and in to the death. So we had won after all! The fate of Hitler and Mussolini's was sealed. The Japanese would be ground to powder."

That was good news for not only those in Somerville, but for all Americans. Most of that Sunday was spent speculating about what would happen next. How was this going to personally affect our own families? Would our sons be called to fight in this war? Many older men recalled the tragic events they had experienced in WWI. They had been through the devastation of the deep Depression years. President Roosevelt has certainly been the man for that time. Did he have the wisdom and courage to lead us in a War? There were many questions with few answers.

Very few homes were seen with all their lights out that night. There were many pots of coffee brewing. Then the morning came.

On Monday, FDR signed the declaration of war granted by Congress. One day later both Germany and Italy, partners of Japan in the Tripartite Pact, declared war on the US.

December 8, 1941, President Roosevelt made his case in his speech to the Congress of the United States.

"Yesterday, Dec. 7, 1941, a date which will live in infamy, the United States of America was suddenly and deliberately attacked by naval and air forces of the Empire of Japan."

"The United States was at peace with that nation and, the solicitation of Japan, was still in conversation with the government and its emperor looking toward the maintenance of peace in the Pacific."

"Indeed, one hour after Japanese air squadrons had commenced bombing in Oahu, the Japanese ambassador to the United States and his colleagues delivered to the Secretary of State a formal reply to a recent American message. While this reply stated that it seemed useless to continue the existing diplomatic negotiations, it contained no threat or hint of war or armed attack."

"It will be recorded that the distance of Hawaii from Japan makes it obvious that the attack was deliberately planned many days or even weeks ago. During the intervening time, the Japanese government has deliberately sought to deceive the United States by false statements and expressions of hope for continued peace."

"The attack yesterday on the Hawaiian Islands has caused severe damage to American naval and military forces. Very many American lives have been lost. In addition, American ships have been reported torpedoed on the high seas between San Francisco and Honolulu."

"Yesterday, the Japanese government also launched an attack against Malaya.

Last night, Japanese forces attacked Hong Kong.

Last night, Japanese forces attacked Guam.

Last night, Japanese forces attacked the Philippine Islands.

Last night, Japanese attacked Wake Island.

This morning, the Japanese attacked Midway Island."

"Japan has, therefore, undertaken a surprise offensive extending throughout the Pacific area. The facts of yesterday speak for themselves. The people of the United States have already formed their opinions and well understand the implications to the very life and safety of our nation."

"As commander in chief of the Army and Navy, I have directed that all measures be taken for our defense."

"Always will we remember the character of the onslaught against us."

"No matter how long it may take us to overcome this premeditated invasion, the American people in their righteous might will win through to absolute victory."

"I believe I interpret the will of the Congress and of the people when I assert that we will not only defend ourselves to the uttermost, but will make very certain that this form of treachery shall never endanger us again."

"Hostilities exist. There is no blinking at the fact that our people, our territory and our interest are in grave danger."

"With confidence in our armed forces, with the unbending determination of our people, we will gain the inevitable triumph, so help us God."

"I ask that the Congress declare that since the unprovoked and dastardly attack by Japan on Sunday, Dec. 7, a state of war has existed between the United States and the Japanese empire."

In spite of the shock waves that enveloped each soul, they knew they needed to gather together at the Church. If ever they needed God's strength and wisdom, it was this day. The Pastor's prepared sermon was set aside. It was time for prayer. Never had they needed to know the presence of God more than they did at this time.

Monday came and work places closed their doors. Families found some sense of security as they huddled together sharing their fears and feelings at home. Some gathered at Kern's café, the spit and whittlers sat on their bench, the hair appointments brought many women to LaShell's Beauty Shop, and other men met at the local pool hall. Life looked as though things were normal. The difference was that the conversation was the same in each of these places. The enormity of the global significance of the Japanese invasion made all the incidental stuff seem as though they were of no value. The question in the minds of the young and old, rich and poor, male and female, black and white was, "What can I do for my country? What will I be called upon to sacrifice for freedom?" Answers to these questions were frightening because of the many unknown factors. These people had just come through the deep depression that followed World War I. The older folks still struggled with memories of those hopeless years. Fortunately, they had learned that when everything looks hopeless you realize you have to look up and trust in God Who has promised He would never leave you or forsake you. They knew from experience that God is the God of the impossible. Nothing is too hard for Him. Different ones would share these promises as they came to their minds. Instinctively most of them knew that their deliverance would come from God as He gave wisdom to their President. Franklin Delano Roosevelt was in that office for just such a time as this.

Fear would turn to faith and calm would settle on those who believed. However, even believers found that it was not long before their faith was tested by what they would hear reported on the radios and in the newsreels in the local theatre. Inevitably, they would easily find a shift from faith back to fear. Even the strongest Christians admitted that this was true in their own lives.

Chapter 2

With the stress of Sunday's news heavy on his heart, Philippe Deriveaux sat on his veranda overlooking the Mississippi River the entire night after hearing F.D.R.'s speech. His dreams of providing his family with the best life that wealth could afford seemed to be shattered. Fifteen years had passed since their move from France to Somerville. With its rich soil, his plantation had produced enough cotton to make him a very wealthy man. He had gained the respect of people throughout Mississippi and neighboring states.

Filled with dreams all those years ago, he brought his family to a place that he felt would enrich the lives of each member. Little did he know that he would, instead, see the breakdown of his precious family. His beautiful wife, Arianne, had been the essence of a life filled excitement about each day. Not long after her move to this quiet lifestyle in Somerville, she had become a recluse, confining herself to her bedroom. There had not been a single day that she had not secretly longed for her European roots. Adjusting to the simple life in Mississippi, where there was such a lack of formal entertaining, she descended into deep depression. She felt that she was in a pit where there was no light, just darkness. Her husband had tried everything to bring joy back into her life. All that his wealth could buy was lavished on her. Their magnificent villa, an exact duplicate of the one she loved in France, had been carefully built just for her. Trips to nearby Memphis were made in order for her to enjoy the theatre and opera performances. Shopping trips were frequent in their early years in Somerville. Yearly trips were made back to France to select her clothes from the most famous couturiers. Most of her time was spent visiting her family in Vienna, Austria. Inevitably, she would have to pack her things and return to Somerville. The sadness became increasingly more evident. Physicians had done their best to try and diagnose her problem. Physically, she was the picture of health. What could possibly be causing this pain? She had no desire to dress and come downstairs to eat with the family. Eating was abhorrent to her. Intimacy had not been an option for Philippe and Arianne for some time.

As Philippe pondered the dilemma, his mind took him back to the early days in France. His thoughts went back to how this move came about. The question haunted him, "Did I make a mistake? Was I wrong in thinking America was the safest place for my children to grow up?

In the midst of his deep thought, dozing occasionally through the night, he was startled to hear Eliza, their treasured housekeeper say, "Lordy mercy, Mr. Deriveaux. Whatcha doing out here in dis cold? You looks like you is worn out. Come on in here to the kitchen and let me fix you some hot coffee to warm you up. I'm gwina git that pot on and then git you a warm blanket to git that chill offin you."

Jolted out of the past and into the present, Philippe humbly complied with Eliza's demands. Shortly after,

Arianne came to the kitchen looking for her husband. Seeing him wrapped in a blanket was not like him at all. "My Darling, are you ill?" Philippe reassured her, "Dearest Arianne, please don't worry. I am fine. My mind was filled with memories. They took me back to our move from France to Somerville. I have pondered the events of these last years trying to make some sense out of all the joys and sorrows we have experienced. Come and sit with me. I need to feel the comfort of your presence."

Philippe's mind could not rest. He began reminding his wife of the beginning of their plans to leave France. "Do you remember when my cousin, Jean Paul, was visiting from New Orleans? He was sharing his excitement about this new country and all its opportunities and challenges with us. The adventurous enthusiasm grasped my spirit. After Jean Paul returned to America, I continued to dream about having such an adventure. You were terrified at the prospect of another move. It was hard for you to leave your beloved family in Austria when we married. Now I was asking you to travel a continent plus an ocean further away from your family. I finally wore down your resistance by assuring you that I would have more time to be with you and the children on the plantation. I would not be constantly leaving home on business trips. With your hesitant submission, I wrote Jean Paul and asked him to search out a suitable plantation. He agreed to help me."

Eliza interrupted once again saying, "Now Mr. Deriveaux, you just keep sittin' there and relax. Miss Arianne, here's you a hot cup of coffee. Now I'm gonna cook up some of those apple fritters you like so much. Everthins gonna be jus fine. Now you know Eliza don't tell nothin' but

9

the truth. The Lord is gonna show us all how to git through this. Now what we gotta do is keep on lookin up."

Philippe went back almost two decades and recalled the story of how Jean Paul visited Memphis, Tennessee, on business. On his way back to New Orleans, he stopped at a pretty little community called Somerville in northwest Mississippi. He asked some of the businessmen if they might know of a plantation for sale. He was told that he was indeed in luck. Mr. Charlie Adams died several months earlier. Not one of his children had any desire to work the land. They all had their own ambitions, and were pursuing them outside of Mississippi. Jean Paul got all the information together and notified me immediately. It was necessary to act quickly. The go ahead was given and arrangements were made with Mr. Adams' heirs for me to buy the plantation.

He told how news spread through Somerville that they were about to receive a new family all the way from Europe. Imaginations were going wild as the townspeople tried to unravel the mystery of what they could expect from foreigners. Not many new families had ever moved into this community. The land had passed down from one generation to another for two hundred years. If it had not been for Mr. Charlie Adams dying, there would not have been a plantation for sale.

While Jean Paul was in Somerville, he met Ephraim Chandler, a wealthy plantation owner. Ephraim was also the president of the Mississippi National Bank of Somerville.

The lawyer of Ephraim's choice and his bank worked out all the business details. Jean Paul was Philippe's liaison.

He remembered Jean Paul telling him about the gracious hospitality of Ephraim who invited him to join his family that evening for dinner. Upon arriving, he was impressed by the line of cedar trees on both sides of the long drive from the road up to their home. Their house was a beautiful Georgian manse, built with red bricks made at Ephraim's brickyard. A double portico painted bright white seemed to welcome its visitor. Before Jean Paul could knock on the door with the big brass doorknocker, the door opened as though someone were standing in the window waiting for his arrival. "Come right on in, Mr. Deriveaux," said their maid, Ella. Dressed in a starched gray and white uniform, her perky personality put a smile on Jean Paul's face and an extra spring in his step.

"Miss Charlotte is waiting for you in the parlor." As he entered the parlor, he was warmly received by Charlotte Chandler. She was the epitome of the gracious southern hostess. Jean Paul was surprised to see "Miss Charlotte", as even her husband lovingly called her, busy at work arranging flowers for the occasion. "Welcome to our home, Mr. Deriveaux. We have looked forward to meeting you. Ephraim will be home any time now. Please come into the parlor. Ella will bring us some of her delicious mint tea." John Paul tried to keep from staring at Charlotte. She was a beautiful woman, with dark brown hair pulled back in a French twist. Her big sparkling brown eyes seemed to embrace each person in her presence. Flawless complexion with a touch of rose in her cheeks and bright red lipstick on her full lips was perfection. She was eloquently dressed in a ruffled white lace blouse and a straight black skirt that accentuated her slim figure. She captivated this Frenchman. With her gracious southern charm, she made you feel at ease, like a member of their family immediately.

Charlotte introduced John Paul to their children: Daisy, 15; Benjamin, 13; Ruth, 12; Samuel, 10; and Phoebe, 7. The daughters were as beautiful as their mother, and the sons, as handsome as their father. Jean Paul complimented Charlotte on the way she had raised her children. Their manners were impeccable and had to be the result of their mother's influence. It was not long before Ephraim arrived home from a business meeting at the church. After greeting his new friend, he gave his wife and each of his children an affectionate hug and kiss. John Paul wanted to remember every detail in order to help his cousin Philippe know how welcomed they were going to be when they arrived.

He remembered how Ella took delight in informing everyone that dinner was ready. And, how funny it sounded when Jean Paul imitated Ella saying, "I hope you got a good appetite 'cause Odeal's done cooked up a mess of food that's gonna make you slap yo' Momma." Charlotte followed with, "Ella, where in the world did you come up with such a saying as that? I never cease to be amazed at the pictures you paint with your words. Mr. Deriveaux, you will find that she is truthful about Odeal's cooking. Let's go and enjoy the food and the fellowship with our new friend", said Charlotte, laughingly.

The aroma from the kitchen had permeated the entire house. They made their way to the large formal dining room. The oversized black walnut furniture had been made for the Chandlers. It was a gift from Ephraim to Charlotte on their wedding day. He knew how she loved to entertain friends around her table. There was the most beautiful black walnut breakfront that had intricate burl inlays and hand carved roses on the doors. It was a breathtaking piece, made in Germany, and left to them in Charlotte's favorite Aunt's will. Beautiful china, Waterford crystal and an assortment of antique pieces filled its glass fronted shelves. A hunt board displayed ornate silver serving dishes that had been passed down through several generations.

Odeal, their treasured cook had indeed prepared a meal fit for a king. Ephraim seated his wife; Jean Paul seated the oldest daughter, Daisy; Benjamin seated his sister, Ruth; and Samuel seated his little sister, Phoebe. Miss Charlotte rang the silver bell to let Odeal know that they were ready to be served. This gave Ephraim just enough time to ask them to bow their heads while he gave thanks to the Lord for their food. "Dear Father, Our hearts are filled with gratitude to You for all your benefits toward us. We thank you for bringing our new friend, Jean Paul, to our home. Our prayer is that You will bless him through us this evening. Now please bless this food to our bodies. Strengthen us that we might better serve you. In Jesus Name we pray. Amen."

Odeal served her soup specialty, creamy peanut butter soup. Jean Paul knew very little about peanut butter, much less about this variety of soup. It did not take long for the Chandlers to see that Odeal had won him over. Taking away the soup bowls, she then returned with the main course. She filled the servers with thick slices of Virginia ham covered with a raisin sauce. Fresh green beans with almonds, sweet potato casserole, and a perfect corn pudding completed the menu. Of course, Odeal had corn bread for the vegetables and always made her homemade yeast rolls that would melt in your mouth. Ice tea with mint was served with the meal and rich Louisiana coffee was served with dessert. Now the best part of the meal was the last surprise…Odeal's famous pecan pie! Needless to say, everyone agreed that it was going to be impossible to move from the dining room to the parlor. With accolades to Odeal, they did somehow manage to move on and even have an extra cup of coffee.

There were so many things Jean Paul needed to tell them about his family. First, he told them that they would not be moving to Somerville until their new home was completed.

Mr. Charlie's house, barn and other buildings would have to be torn down. Everything was to be new from the ground up. Many things would be imported from France and Italy. He told them about how difficult it was going to be for them to make this move. He told of how excited they were about the new start for their family. But Arienne certainly did not share Philippe's adventurous spirit. He told them that she had been born into Austrian royalty. Her life had been caught up in the glamorous lifesyle of European society. He told them that while in Austria on government business, he was introduced to a beautiful Austrian princess at a royal gala. He was swept away by her poise and beauty and vivacious personality. It was while they were dancing, that they realized there was an intense mutual attraction. He told us that as they danced across the ballroom floor, they still remembered that they felt as though they were floating. He had even extended his trip two more weeks so that he could spend more time getting to know her. Completely convinced that fate had brought them together, they committed themselves to each other after a short time. A few months later, with both of their families in complete agreement with the union, plans were put into motion for the wedding that would impress all of European society. Engraved invitations were hand delivered by messenger service.

In September of 1895, at a large cathedral in Vienna, family and friends arrived to celebrate with them as they exchanged vows to one another before God. After the ceremony they were treated to a cruise around the Greek Islands on a lavish yatch. This was a gift to them from Aristotle Stephanophilos, a wealthy Greek shipping tycoon. He recalled the storm they encountered just before their return from the islands to Paris. The terrifying experience convinced Arianne that she was safe in her husband's strong arms. Returning home to France, they settled into a villa that had been in the family for several hundred years. They loved their new home. Each day seemed to bring this young couple closer and more in love. But the day came when Arianne began to feel homesick for her family in Austria. Philippe was often away from home on business trips leaving her with servants and friends of his family who had never quite accepted the fact that he did not marry one of their own. The French people were very open with their feelings. This made Arianne extremely uncomfortable.

One year after their wedding, his beautiful Arianne gave birth to their first child, Edmond. Philippe was ecstatic over having a son and an heir to carry on the Deriveaux name. Edmond was three when Arianne gave birth to their second son, Charles. She longed to have a little girl so that she could teach all the special feminine things that meant so much to her. Her desire was fulfilled when she gave birth to Celeste, and then two years later, they welcomed Vivian into their family. Their last child was born two years after Vivian. He was the third son, Armond. He would complete the family. Each one brought such joy to their lives. Oh, the memories the children had given them! Some sad but many still blessed their hearts today.

After telling the Chandlers about their soon to be new neighbors, Jean Paul proceeded to take care of some of the necessary business details. They had to have the best building contractor in the south. Ephraim knew about a man in Huntsville, Alabama, Bill Michael, who had a reputation for building palatial homes. He contacted him and was given the name of a contractor in Memphis who had studied with Bill for many years. He assured Jean Paul that the home would be in the best of hands. The villa had to be built to detailed specifications. Marble, chandeliers and other appointments would be shipped from Europe. When completed, it would be as though no one else had ever lived on this piece of land. This would ultimately annoy many of the local people. After all, was this foreigner too uppity for them? How dare he act like Mr. Charlie's place wasn't special enough for him? Ephraim and Charlotte had a job ahead of them trying to keep the gossip level down to a minimum. Why, even their church members were buzzing about these high and mighty people.

Chapter 3

After the basic problems involved in building the villa and the landscape details were worked out, there was one more problem to solve. Jean Paul inquired as to who might be available to work for him. They would need a trustworthy staff of servants. Positions would be available for a chauffeur who would also serve as a butler, a cook, a housekeeper, and someone to oversee the plantation. He was lucky to find a family large enough to fill all of these jobs. Henry Jones would be the ideal man to oversee the plantation. He was a ten year old son of a slave at the end of the civil war. He remembered well the abominable treatment of slaves especially when it seemed imminent that they were going to get their freedom granted to them by law. Upon release from slavery, they were given a piece of land. Henry's father was a hard working man who taught his son a valuable work ethic. Henry's mother taught him the most wonderful truth in the world. She instilled in her children that a man might hate you for no better reason than that your skin is a different color, but God loves you and values you because he created you in His own image. She reminded him daily that just because someone does and says demeaning things to you, it does not make these things truth. He learned very early that he was to search for truth in the Holy Bible. He could rest on every promise he found there because God will never lie.

Henry met a precious, godly young woman one day at a church meeting. Her name was Eliza. Their love for each other was too strong to wait, and their commitment to God was too real for them to just give into their feelings, so they married one month after they met. Both their families agreed that this was a match made in Heaven. God's blessing was on them from the beginning.

Henry and Eliza Jones wanted to have a large family. God gave them six wonderful children: John, who they called "Big John", came into this world weighing a whopping twelve pounds, six ounces. He grew up to be 6 feet, 7 inches tall, and weighed about three hundred and fifty pounds, and it was all muscle. James was their second son. Their earliest memories made them know that he was going to be musically gifted. He was singing in their church services by the time he was three years old. Mary was their first little girl. She was headstrong from the beginning, always asking, "Why?" about everything. There was no sign of a subservient attitude in this child. Since these were the times in the south when even though you were not slaves, you still were not free to express yourself openly. You were to know your place and stay in it. Henry and Eliza lived in fear of how Mary would ever survive with her sharp tongue. Luke was the next child born. He was premature, and since there was inadequate medical care available to a black family with little money and no insurance, his lungs and heart were weak all of his life. Sarah followed Luke in the birth order. She was their prettiest child, and grew up to look like a tall, thin model.

What concerned Henry and Eliza about Sarah was that all the men, black and white, could not keep from gazing upon her beauty. She seemed to thoroughly enjoy the attention. The last pregnancy was very difficult for Eliza. She awoke one morning to discover that she was severely swollen. Henry took her to the doctor who said that she had toxemia. Her albumin count was very high and her blood pressure was dangerously high. She had to have complete bed rest. Fortunately for her, the other children were old enough by now to take over the chores. In the eighth month, a midwife delivered another boy, Little Henry. The premature baby weighed only three pounds. The mid-wife wrapped him in a blanket and placed him near the wood stove to keep him very warm. Bricks were heated to give extra heat. God must have sent angels to watch over him, because he survived against great odds. Eliza's blood pressure came back down as soon as she delivered Little Henry. He never grew up to be great in stature, only five foot, five inches tall, but he grew into a spiritual giant. His love for Jesus was so deep. Early in his life it was clear that God's plan for Little Henry was to preach His Good News, the Gospel of Jesus Christ to the multitudes. What a foundation he had being privileged to grow up in this spiritual environment.

When Henry was approached about working for the Deriveaux's, he was thrilled to learn that there were jobs for all the members of his family. He would oversee the plantation. Eliza would be the housekeeper and cook. Big John would double as the chauffer and tender of the stables. James was given the job of butler and valet. Mary and Sarah would work under Eliza's supervision as maids and cooks. Luke was unable to do anything strenuous, so he was given the job of taking care of Little Henry. It was Luke who taught Little Henry to read using the Bible as the text, and thus instilling the precious word of God into this future preacher's heart.

It seemed that Ellen came out of her shy shell after Hannah arrived. There was an awareness that came to her showing her that she truly was special. That had never dawned on her before. Instead of hiding in corners reading her books she began to write her own book. She looked into her soul and saw many different characters with manifold experiences and personalities. It was not difficult to feel their pain as she had experienced so much personally. It freed her to write about the beautiful extrovert as she found herself living vicariously through her. Words and thoughts flowed from her heart through the pen to the page. She had found her personal passion. Like a butterfly being released from its cocoon she could finally fly.

Ellen showed some of her pages to her Mother. "Mama", she sighed, "I felt like a butterfly that was trapped. It saw a window and the glass appeared to be a place of escape. But when the butterfly hit the glass it could go no further. Its wings flapped as hard as they could but got nowhere. It flew from one side of the window to the other making no progress. The wings grew weaker. Suddenly someone opened a door. With all the urging the butterfly just kept trying to make it on its own. Then the deliverer took the weak butterfly and gently picked it up and carried it to the open door. With loving-kindness, he said, *Fly, little Butterfly, fly!* You are free to be and do what you were created to do.

Mama, I believe that God used Hannah to somehow help me to see that if that little German butterfly could be set free then so could I. I'm supposed to write. I don't know whether anyone will ever want to publish or read my book. But I know that I've got to write it. This little butterfly is going to take this opportunity to quit hiding in a corner thinking I'm a failure just flapping my wings against a window. I plan to fly from now on!"

Millicent took her precious little girl in her strongest embrace. Speaking through her tears, she said, "My darling Ellen, you have always been a joy to your mother. I have known since the days you were in my womb that God had a plan for you. It hurt me deeply to see you try to hide the real Ellen for fear of failure or rejection. All the years of hiding in your books were not a waste of time. It just prepared you for this moment the awareness of your writing *gift*. I am proud of you and can't wait to sit by your side when book reviewers give you the rewards you richly deserve."

Chapter 4

Thomas Scott Middleton owned the plantation to the south of the Deriveaux's.

Thomas was an austere man who had acquired his wealth by being a successful cotton grower and sheep rancher. He supplied clothing factories across the south with cotton and wool. Thomas was not born to wealth. This explained his dislike for people like the Deriveaux's who he believed had gotten everything handed to them on a silver platter. He had fought and scratched for every material thing he had. Thomas' father was a drunk. With few skills, he took jobs wherever he could find them. The pittance that he made was immediately spent on cheap wine. Thomas' mother worked hard in the fields for pitiful wages. At least that was used to buy necessities for her children. The people she worked for knew her circumstances and would see that she had vegetables from their gardens and milk from their cows.

When Thomas was fifteen years old, he ran away from home. He stowed away on a Mississippi river boat. The Captain of the boat, Rick Rogers, discovered his runaway and was going to throw him off the boat at the next stop. Thomas was able to persuade him that he had no family, and that he would not survive out on the streets in some strange place. The Captain had sons of his own, and this sad tale caused him to think again about what to do with Thomas. "Okay," he said, "You can stay with us but you will have to work for your keep. You will get up early in the morning and scrub the decks. You will have chores in the galley helping with food preparation. When we dock, you will help carry cargo from the boat to the dock and from the dock back to the boat. Other jobs will be assigned to you as they come up. You will work harder than you have ever worked in your life, and I don't want any lip from you. Is that understood?" "Yes, sir," Thomas said timidly, not knowing what he had gotten himself into.

For the next three years, Thomas grew up knowing little apart from the river boat lifestyle. He did, indeed, learn how to work hard. As tough as Captain Rogers was, Thomas knew that he owed him a debt of gratitude for shaping his future. After the three years, he had saved enough from his wages to buy a little piece of land outside of Somerville. There was a little house on a hill that he was able to call his own. When he returned home, he found out, he found out that his father had gotten into a fight when he was in one of his drunken state. The other man pulled a hunting knife from his jacket and plunged it into his father's heart. His worthless body was carried off to a desolate place. A hole was dug and his body was thrown in without a proper burial or a single mourner.

After the death of his mother and father, and the responsibility of care of his two brothers and one sister, Thomas found happiness in meeting a young woman named Millicent Perkins. The two of them could not have been more opposite. She was a polite "church going lady." Thomas did not even believe in God and was anything but courteous. He instinctively saw that she could be a help to him. Thomas had no social skills, and had great difficulty interacting with businessmen; but he seemed to have the Midas touch and was acquiring more land each year. His little land purchase soon became a plantation to be reckoned with. What he needed now was a touch of grace. Millicent could compliment him in that area.

Millicent knew that Thomas was crude and was an unbeliever so she resisted his requests to go out on a date. Finally he realized that if he was ever going to get to first base with her, it was going to have to be by way of making her think he was at least interested in going with her to church. She was thrilled that he seemed to be showing some sign of repenting from his harsh ways.

The following Sunday he walked with her into the small First Baptist Church in their little town of Somerville. The organ was playing some highbrow thing that bored him to death. Some woman got up to sing a solo. The noise level seemed to pierce his eardrums. The offering plate was passed. He realized Millicent was looking to see what he would do. He was forced to reach into his pocket and put a five-dollar bill in the plate. Now he was feeling claustrophobic. The preacher walked to the podium and opened his large Bible. "The text for today is taken from Romans 3:23, 'For all have sinned and come short of the glory of God.'" The beads of sweat popped out on Thomas' head. He wanted to run away like he had done when he was fifteen. But he knew that would be the end of his chance to win Millicent, and he needed her to be his wife. Somehow he stayed in his pew, but he heard nothing else that day except, "All have sinned." One thing he knew for sure was that he wanted no part of this church life. He kept that from Millicent. He convinced her that he was a seeker of the Truth. Thinking she could help him come to God, she agreed to marry Thomas. He was very good at saying what someone wanted to hear in order to get what he wanted. He even talked the Minister into marrying them in a small wedding ceremony. He took his bride to his home, which had been added on as he became more affluent. From the very beginning, because of his own insecurities, he had a difficult time with feelings of love and expressing his emotions. Millicent felt unloved from their wedding night. This created in her a sense of unworthiness. Her self-esteem hit rock bottom. What had she done wrong? Her husband seemed to want a servant instead of a wife. To Thomas, a sexual relationship with his wife was strictly for the purpose of procreation. Many were the nights when Millicent felt used and abused, and there was never a time when Thomas just held her in his arms and expressed his love for her.

Their marriage produced six children: Thomas, Jr. who grew up to hate his father for the way he treated his mother. He despised the fact that he was burdened with his father's name. He insisted on being called "Hoss." He felt that was what his father expected him to be, an animal fit only to work the fields.

The second child was a girl, Ellen, who was painfully shy from the earliest years. They thought she might be deaf because she did not seem to respond to anyone. As she grew older, she retreated into books. The only outward behavior her family saw was when someone interrupted her reading.

It would make her so angry; she would throw something at the intruder.

William was the third child. He was sensitive as Hoss was hardened. He loved to join his mother in the kitchen when she was cooking. He wanted to learn how to prepare sumptuous meals and he put such emphasis on the presentation. Millicent loved the closeness they had together in the kitchen. However, Thomas was infuriated at the prospect that one of his sons had such a feminine side. He took every opportunity to ridicule him. William knew that he would never be able to please his father so he tried avoid spending time in his presence.

Priscilla was a born athlete. When she could not be found, they knew that she was out running somewhere. It was nothing for her to run six miles a day. Somehow running, whether in cold weather or hot, seemed to make her feel a freedom that she could not explain. It was something she had to do, and she did it even when she knew she would receive her father's wrath for not working in the fields every spare minute.

Lawrence was born next. Maybe it was because he had the older siblings and was able to feel secure in their love that he seemed to be more content in his circumstances, in spite of his father, who was expressing his anger more and more. There were times that the children would hear him cursing their mother and they knew that he would even strike her. She would be very careful to cry her tears in a private place to keep from involving the children. At all cost, she wanted to keep Hoss from feeling like he had to defend her. She knew that one of them could easily be killed.

Melanie was the last child born to Thomas and Millicent. She was a little china doll with beautiful blond hair and pink complexion and big blue eyes. All the children felt like she was a doll to cherish and play with. Millicent needed the help with her care. She had been through such pain for so long. Her health was bad. High blood pressure was the result of the years of stress under which she had lived.

When the children were in their teens, Thomas told Millicent that he was fed up with all of them. They were all losers. He wanted a divorce, and they all would have to leave his house. He told her that they were going to have to move into a small, run down house across a large field from the big house. Millicent begged him not to force the children to live in such horrible conditions. How would they ever survive? Her pleas fell on deaf ears. Thomas told her that he was going to let all of them work the fields. They would have a roof over their heads and a portion of the produce that they would raise for him to sell. They would pick the cotton with the other hired hands. Thomas hired a lawyer who was not opposed to be bribed. He forced Millicent into agreeing to the divorce and getting absolutely nothing for all the years she spent with this worthless excuse for a husband. Millicent feared for her life and for her children's lives, and so she signed the divorce papers.

The shanty they called home now had cracks in the walls that allowed the wind to blow through with a loud whistling noise. It was freezing cold in the winter, and equally as hot in the summer. For cold weather, there was a potbelly stove used for heat and for cooking. Hoss cut the wood for the stove. All the children were expected to gather wood and bring it into the house. Melanie, the baby, would cry and beg her mother not to make her go into the cold. Her hand would surely freeze. All the crying did not keep her from having to assume at least a little bit of responsibility. Everyone was expected to do something. Their light was from oil lanterns. There was an outhouse and a well from which they drew their water. The anger and bitterness grew deep into the hearts of all the children.

The heaviness of Millicent's plight continually drove her to her knees. There was no one else to turn to expect her God. Her personal relationship with her Heavenly Father through His Son, Jesus Christ, was indeed her salvation. She was diligent in her prayer life. Bible Study was never neglected. She needed daily to search God's Word to find encouragement and strength. Every night, before they went to sleep, she would read Scriptures to her children, planting that precious Word in their hearts. Each child joined her in a personal prayer. Peaceful sleep was their reward from God. Each morning, as they began their day with a bowl of oatmeal, a biscuit and milk, they would all hold hands, thank God for His watch care over them, and ask Him to keep them safe throughout the day.

One day they looked up on the hill and saw several carpenters working on the big white house they used to live in. Day after day, they saw the columns repaired, the roof replaced and the house painted with bright white paint and emerald green shutters.

Millicent heard through the community gossip vine that Thomas was getting married again. Much to her surprise, he had gone to Memphis on some business trips.

There he met a beautiful, young blond woman, whose name was Benita. What he felt for her was pure lust because he had no heart. She saw her opportunity to marry an older man who promised her the world. There was only one hitch. Benita was the younger half-sister of Millicent. They did not really know each other well. Millicent's father died and her mother moved to Memphis. There she met and married her second husband. Benita was the child born in this marriage.

After Thomas and Benita's wedding, he brought her back to the beautiful white two-story home on the hill. A lavish reception was given to introduce Benita to Somerville society. The Deriveauxs and the Chandlers were invited. But Millicent and the children were relegated to looking up from their destitute environment and seeing such opulence. The pain and hurt and hate meshed together. They clung to each other and cried together. Hoss yelled out, "There will be a special Hell for Thomas Middleton."

God ministered to Millicent and her children through many Godly people. Henry and Eliza Jones were friends of theirs who were always ready to help them. Ephraim and Charlotte Chandler knew their plight. The church had prayed for them and cared for them through the years. Millicent knew that she could always count on all of them to be there for her family if they reached a place where they could not go on. But above all, Millicent knew God would always be faithful to His Word. He promised to provide for all their needs according to His riches in Glory by Christ Jesus. She learned to lean on Him when times were so hard.

Millicent became a very close friend of Eliza Jones. At this time in the south it was almost unheard of that a white person would have as her best friend, a black woman. Each of these women had been born again. Their hearts were filled with God's love that has the power to tear down all the barriers that men had built up. These two women along with Ephraim and Charlotte were all a part of the family of God. That made them brothers and sisters in Christ. All of these friends had to tread lightly in this place of Mississippi during such a time as this.

Chapter 5

As Philippe and Arianne continued to reminisce about their early days in Somerville, he recalled the long wait before they moved into their new home. It had taken many builders a little over a year to complete the construction of their magnificent dream home. The results were overwhelmingly successful. The architectural design was Mediterranean. Large marble columns were situated across the front of the villa. The back of the villa was as beautiful as the front. A veranda, the width of the house, extended out from the four French Doors. The house was built on a bluff overlooking the Mississippi River. Steps went down from the veranda to a second level with an Olympic size swimming pool. A beautiful gazebo was off to the side of the pool. Urns with fragrant flowers were in full bloom. Magnolia and oak trees provided shade in the hot summers. When the magnolias were in bloom their delicate sweet aroma filled the air. Philippe was gazing on the perfection of it all. Looking at the ornate table and comfortable chairs, he had flashes of memory of their first days on the plantation.

The move from France had gone quite well. Arianne was in agreement that this was the beginning of a new life for all of them. It seemed to be a good time to leave Europe. World War I was threatening the safety of France and Austria along with a large part of Europe and the United States. There were mixed emotions about leaving their families. At the same time it was the best thing for the entire family. Arianne walked through the massive hand carved doors with their beautiful etched beveled glass at the top and felt right at home. The marble columns, steps and porch floors captured her heart. This was indeed the beauty of Europe even if it was in the Mississippi Delta. Philippe breathed a sigh of relief to see that she was going to be happy at last.

Upon their arrival in Somerville, Henry Jones greeted them at their car. Jean Paul, Philippe's cousin, had briefed them thoroughly as to the different ones who would serve them. Philippe knew that Henry was the overseer of the plantation. Everyone who worked for the Deriveauxs would answer to him. He introduced himself and his oldest son, John, to their new employer. They took them into the house where they met Henry's wife, Eliza. He addressed Arianne, "Mrs. Deriveaux, this is my wife, Eliza, who will take care of the matters concerning the household." Other members of the Jones family were introduced to the Deriveauxs. Everyone was ready to do his or her assigned jobs. This family's warmth and dignity put the Deriveauxs completely at ease. Things could not have worked out any better. Wonderful years were in store for this family from France.

The first years were filled with excitement. Soon laughter turned to sadness and hope turned to despair.

Arianne seemed to be turning inward and spending more and more time in her bedroom.

Reality set into Philippe's memory when it went back to the worse day of his life. It seemed like a normal morning until he heard Eliza screaming for him, "Mr. Deriveaux, come quickly. Miss Arianne won't wake up!"

Philippe ran into the house and up the massive staircase, racing down the long hall to the master bedroom. Eliza was following as fast as she could. He broke into a cold sweat when he saw his beloved wife's lifeless body. "Arianne, wake up." He tried slapping her face and putting cold water on her face, but there was no response. "Eliza, call Big John. Then call the doctor and tell him to meet us at the hospital."

While waiting for Big John, Philippe spotted an empty bottle of pills on the floor beside the bed. The doctor had prescribed something to help her sleep and something for her depression. He didn't know which pills she had taken. It had been such a long time since she had confided in her husband about anything.

Big John came running up the stairs, taking two steps at a time and ran into the bedroom. Philippe was cradling his wife in his arms. Tears were streaming from his eyes. Over and over he kept repeating, "God, please don't let her die. Please don't take her from me. I know I have not had any time for you in my life before. I promise you that I will do whatever you want me to do if you will only let her live."

Big John took her from his arms and carried her down the stairs as if she were a baby. He drove to the hospital as fast as the car would go. Dr. Wilkins was waiting for them. He immediately pumped her stomach and successfully emptied it of the threatening overdose.

Philippe said, "I cannot bear leaving her in this small hospital." Dr. Wilkins agreed to let us take her home as long as I would hire his nurse to stay with her overnight. Upon returning home with my weak, frail Arianne, I was reminded by Eliza of what I had promised God.

Arianne and I had known that Henry, Eliza and their children were committed Christians. Although they were living testimonies to their faith, they did not feel that they could impose their beliefs on their employers. Many times Arianne would open a door that would allow Eliza to share her faith. It was not long before the freedom to keep on sharing was just not there. Arianne's medication caused her to drift off in the midst of a conversation. Eliza had learned to back off and pray for another open door in the near future.

Philippe began to talk to Henry and Eliza seriously about God. Religion in France was formal and non-personal. The large cathedrals were filled with statues, but there was no life in these statues. In fact, there were very few people who actually went to Mass there. When they did attend, it seemed as though it was nothing more than mere ritual. They left with the same countenance with which they entered. He told them that he honestly never had a desire to even search for God if that was all he would find.

He told Henry and Eliza that he had seen something different in them, even though he knew that they had a history of hard times. Their grandparents were slaves. Their parents were young when they announced the Emancipation Proclamation. Slaves were freed and were given portions of land to give them a new start. Although they had worked extremely hard working their land, they still had so little materially speaking. And yet, he noticed that they always had a sweet smile on their faces. "It is so obvious that the love you have for your family is real and genuine." He told them that he had heard them singing and whistling even when he knew they were dead tired. No matter what, they are always thanking God for His blessings. Philippe asked "How do you do that when it doesn't seem like you have a great number of things to be thankful for?"

Henry said, "Oh, Mr. Deriveaux, God has done been so good to us. It just ain't the same kind of things you think of as blessings. You see, He's given His black children freedom. Now that freedom is sho' nuff from the burden of slavery. But mo' than that, He done set us free from our sin when we asked His sweet Jesus to come into our hearts and save us. You see, when folks has been under the yoke of slavery, there ain't no place to look but up. Black folks was bad off and beat down. They knew inside their souls that the only one who could help them was Jesus. So they just bowed their hearts to Him every day. You see, Mr. Deriveaux, Jesus is the only one who can really satisfy our soul. So we may not have a big house and we ain't got no extra money, just what we need to live on, but we got a promise. And that promise is that Jesus has built us a mansion in Heaven. We is gonna walk with Him on golden streets forever and ever. And that makes us rich folks!"

Philippe continued to remember that he had no place in his thinking for all the things Henry was sharing with him. He thought to himself that someone must have planted all this idealistic future in Henry's mind at an early age. As Phillipe's mind tried to sort through what he was hearing. His heart continued to tell him that there must be some reason why the Jones family had such peace and joy. I told Henry that I would like to continue this conversation with him at a later time. In the meantime, chores had to be done and Henry was excused.

After Henry left, I remember putting my head in my hands and weeping uncontrollably. I felt so inadequate to be able to reach my precious wife. I wondered if I had made the biggest mistake of my life when I convinced her to move to Mississippi. Her life had always been wrapped up in extravagant galas and her lavish lifestyle in Europe. Trips to Memphis or New Orleans did not fulfill her desire to be the center of attention. Her beauty had always been on display from the time she was a little girl. Their plantation was like a barren desert by comparison.

The news of Arianne's overdose ran through the small town of Somerville like water through a sieve. As soon as Charlotte Chandler heard about it she immediately went to the Deriveauxs to see if there was anything she could do to help. That was the difference between Charlotte and most of the other women in the church. She had the spiritual gifts of mercy and service. Most of the women in this sleepy town spent more of their time talking about what must have gone wrong to make such a rich lady want to take her life.

Eliza met Charlotte at the door and invited her to come in. "Miss Charlotte, I'm so glad to see you. I think you might be able to help Miss Arianne. She looks up to you cause she knows there's not a phony bone in yo' body. Come with me on up to Miss Arianne's room," said Eliza. They knocked on the door, and the nurse came to see who was there. Eliza asked, "Is Miss Arianne awake so she could see Miss Charlotte?" The nurse replied, "Yes, she is awake. In fact she had just finished drinking a cup of tea and is feeling a little bit better. Come on in."

Charlotte pulled a beautiful Chippendale chair up to the bedside. "Arianne, I am so glad to see that you are feeling better. I felt a need to come to you and see if there is anything I might do for you." With a very soft, weak voice Arianne whispered, "Dear Charlotte, I was hoping you might come by. I have wanted to talk to you for a long time. But I have been so tired and unable to reach out to anyone. I feel like I can't hold my head up or lift my arms. To be truthful, I have just concluded that the best thing for me and for my family would be for me to simply die."

Charlotte took her hand and gently rubbed it. With tears in her eyes, she said, "Oh, Arianne, do you know how loved you are? Philippe adores you. Your children love you so. I love you my friend. But most of all God loves you more than all of us together." Now tears had filled Arianne's eyes. She answered, "God could not possibly love someone like me. I have never given Him any reason to take note of me at all. I have lived my life so selfishly only thinking of what I needed. Until now I have not felt any need for God. Now I know that all my wealth and physical beauty has never really satisfied my deep longing for peace. It's too late now. I can't even think rationally anymore. I stay so medicated that I sleep most of the day. I have shut my husband away from me as much as possible. I insist on the draperies being closed so that I hardly know anymore that light exist. There is no hope for me."

Charlotte asked if she would excuse her for just a minute. She left the room. Eliza was standing outside the door trying ever so hard to hear what they were saying. "Eliza, is there a

Bible in the house somewhere? I need God's word to share with Arianne. She is so ready to hear something that will give her the will to live." Eliza broke out in a big smile and said, "Yes, Ma'm, I keeps a Bible in the kitchen. They ain't much time to read it, but I feel like it's gonna make the Devil think twice about messing with us here. Yes, Ma'm, Miss Arianne is gonna come to Jesus for her help. I just knows she is!" She hurriedly ran down the stairs to get her Bible and quickly returned to the bedroom.

Charlotte opened it to John 3:16, and said, "Listen to this, Arianne. 'For God so loved the world that He gave His only begotten Son that whosoever believes on Him should have everlasting life.' God also said in John 10:10 that He came to give you life, and that life more abundantly."

Arianne could not comprehend these words. She asked, "Does that mean that it's for someone like me in this kind of mess?"

"It most certainly does." All have sinned and come short of the glory of God, but God loved us even while we were sinners." He demonstrated that love when Jesus died on Calvary's cross shedding His precious blood in order to save us from our sin." With a puzzled look on her face Arianne asked what that could possibly mean to her. Charlotte explained to her that God tells us in Romans 6:23, "The wages of sin is death; but the gift of God is eternal life through Jesus Christ, our Lord." She went on to explain to her that we have earned eternal separation from God as a result of our sins. Jesus' death offers us eternal life. It's a free gift of grace from God to anyone who will believe on His Son. Arianne, you have received many priceless gifts in your lifetime. Did you have to work for those gifts?"

"Indeed not," replied Arianne. "That would not have been a gift any longer." "You've got that exactly right," said Charlotte. "The first step is to understand how much God loves you. Then you must desire to receive His gift of salvation by faith. The most amazing thing happens at that point. He delights in giving you a new life, a new beginning place." The biggest smile came across this formally sad face as she, now with a loud voice replied, "Oh, Charlotte that is what I desperately need. A new beginning place sounds like heaven on earth. What must I do to receive God's marvelous gift?"

"God has been right by you waiting patiently for you to cry out to Him. Romans 10:9-10, says 'If you confess with your mouth Jesus as Lord, and believe in your heart that God raised Him from the dead, you shall be saved. For with the heart man believes unto righteousness and with the mouth he confesses, resulting in salvation. In verse 13, He says "whosoever shall call upon the Lord shall be saved.' Arianne, do you understand what that means to you personally?"

"Oh, Charlotte, my heart is pounding. I know somehow this is exactly what had been missing in my life. Can I call on God now and get started on my new life?" Eliza was still standing outside the door. God's spirit just took over and she could not restrain herself. She burst into the room shouting, "Glory to God, Miss Arianne. You is ready for the biggest day of yo life. I wanna git in on it."

Charlotte and Eliza helped Arianne down from her tall poster bed. The three of them knelt before God. Arianne, sobbing and rejoicing at the same time, cried out, "Dear God in Heaven, thank you for loving and caring about me.

I know I have sinned for so long and messed up my life. But I believe that You love me and Your Son died for me. Please forgive me of my sins, and I give You all that I am for the rest of my life. Show me what You want me to do. I'm yours from this day on." Before she finished her prayer, strength replaced weakness; joy replaced sadness. Tears still flowed but now they were tears of joy. She now had a Heavenly Father and that meant she also had two new spiritual sisters and the color of the skin made no difference. The three of them held each other and praised God together.

Charlotte said her good-byes and promised Arianne that she would be back to see her soon. Eliza remained to keep her company while she was adjusting to the change that had just taken place in her life. There were so many questions that she needed answers. However she realized that her immediate need was to get some sleep. Eliza helped her into her bed and gently pulled the covers over her. "Now, Miss Arianne, you just think on sweet Jesus and you is gonna fall asleep fast," she said. Sure enough she was out like a light with the most peaceful look on her beautiful face.

Before Charlotte left their home, she went out to the veranda to speak to Philippe. He jumped up to meet her asking about his wife. "Philippe, you don't have to worry about her anymore. Her search for peace ended today when she met the Prince of Peace personally. She surrendered her life to Jesus Christ just a little while ago. Now she has the power of God in her life. That is what has been missing all this time. She's sleeping right now. Then Eliza will give her some hot soup. You'll see her get stronger and stronger. She has such a glorious future ahead of her. All the longing for her family and her homeland will decrease as she finds complete satisfaction in her Savior." Charlotte continued by explaining to Philippe that even Arianne does not as yet understand all that has happened to her, and asked him to let her tell him a little at a time what she does understand.

Charlotte said, "Philippe, Ephraim and I would like it very much if you and Arianne could come to our home for dinner as soon as she is strong enough. We would like to be there for both of you to share the Word of God with you. As a new Christian Arianne must be spoon fed like a little baby. And our prayer will be that as you listen you will come to see how much God loves you and wants you to come to Him and find your rest in Him. The most beautiful thing in this world is when a husband and wife walk together with Jesus Christ through the rest of their lives. Would you accept our invitation to dinner?"

"I don't understand much of anything that you have said. But I sincerely hope that what you have said about my dear wife is true. She has been desperately unhappy for such a long time. I feared that I had lost her when she took the overdose of pills. If God has indeed spared her and has given her this new beginning place there is nothing I would not do to repay Him," cried Philippe.

Charlotte took his hand and said, "My friend, you could never repay God in material things for what He does for His child. He desires only one thing from you. That is faith and obedience. He longs to give you new birth if you will believe on His Son, Jesus Christ. Then by faith and in obedience you receive Him as your own Lord and Savior. He will do the same thing for you that He has done for Arianne."

Charlotte knew that she had planted the seed of faith. Now she needed to leave Philippe to ponder these truths and hopefully begin a practice of calling on God himself. On her way home she burst out singing,

Amazing Grace, How Sweet the Sound
That Saved a Wretch like Me
I Once Was Lost, but Now I'm Found, was blind but
Now I See.

She knew that this was true in her life, in Eliza's life, and now in Arianne's life. Her spirit rejoiced in God, their Savior!

Chapter 6

After Charlotte left, Philippe once again became lost in his thoughts of the past few years. This time he was focused on the children they had loved so deeply. When they arrived in Somerville, Edmond, their oldest son, was nineteen years old. The political gene had passed down through Philippe. The time for college enrollment was just around the corner. Philippe upon the advice of his new friend Ephraim Chandler drove him to Oxford, Mississippi. Oxford was located in northeastern part of the state so the drive was not too hard.

The University of Mississippi was chosen because of its excellent law school. He planned to get his law degree plus a minor in political science. Then he would work toward a career in politics that hopefully would take him all the way to Washington, D.C. Of course the entire family would have to become citizens of the United States as soon as possible. Philippe was very proud to see his first son following in his footsteps. There was one thing that concerned him. Edmond thought he was God's gift to women. He continually cautioned him to remember to concentrate on his career goals first. Then he could get serious about the young lady who would be his potential wife. It was not easy for Edmond to think in terms of celibacy until after college, law school and marriage. This reckless youth took advantage of young girls who were overwhelmed by his rugged good looks and fascinating French accent.

Charles, their second son, had been the child who had broken their hearts. Their little baby was beautiful and seemed absolutely normal in every way. They began to notice as the months passed that he was not progressing as had his older brother. While in France they took him to the best pediatricians who then referred them to other specialists. After much testing they were told that their son was a savant. He would never develop mentally, emotionally or physically like a normal child. They were urged to put him in an institution for everyone's good. This was unthinkable for Philippe and Arianne. He was their child. It was settled immediately. They would hire the help they needed to care for him. That was a decision they never regretted making.

When Charles was about five years old the sound of music permeated their home. Someone was playing the grand piano in the music room. Arianne went to see who was playing so early in the morning. Much to her surprise it was little Charles. She went over to the piano and sat next to him on the bench. "My sweet child," she said lovingly, "How did you learn to play so beautifully?" He said nothing but continued playing. She could not hold back the tears. God had given him such a special gift. How else could it be explained?

Philippe recalled returning home from his office that evening to find his wife glowing. She said, "Come quickly to the music room. I will get Charles. He has an amazing surprise for you." Soon she returned with Charles. As Philippe waited Charles sat at the piano and began to play as though he had been taking lessons from a master pianist. "How can this be?" asked Philippe. The next day they sought answers from the best doctors in the psychiatric community. These doctors explained that it was not unusual for a savant to be deficient in many skills and in social behavior. Charles was a musical prodigy. Often the individual would be a genius in the area of math or in the ability to even take a watch apart and put all the intricate parts back together again. Charles would bring pain and joy into their family for the rest of his life. Phillipe smiled as he thought back on how thankful he was that he and his wife had refused to give him up to an institution. Charles was sixteen years old when they moved to Somerville.

Philippe's mind turned to their third child. A little girl named Celeste. She was only fourteen when they left France but France never completely left Celeste. From the time she was a little girl her mother had spoiled her with the best of everything money could buy. She went with her mother to fashion shows by the greatest designers from the time she was about three. Her love for clothes grew deeper each year. Many hours were spent in her mother's closets trying on her elegant clothes, high heel shoes, furs and especially the dazzling diamonds. She would rather die than get a speck of dirt on herself.

At fourteen, she knew for sure that she wanted to be a model and a designer. Physically she was born to do just that. She was already five foot, eight inches tall, and had not quit growing. Her thin, willowy frame and her flawless complexion framed by her long silky black hair were breathtaking. Philippe had a sinking feeling in the pit of his stomach as he thought about how he would be able to let her leave Somerville and move to New York City. He feared that the next move would be back to Paris. She was so precious to him.

Then his thoughts changed to Vivian who was only twelve years old. She was their little extrovert. There was no way to describe her except to say that her personality and laughter would dispel any gloom. She never met a stranger. Everyone loved her. They never had to worry about whether she would be accepted in her new school. She would charm the socks off teachers and schoolmates. She could entertain everyone with her sense of humor and her effervescent personality. She often talked about being an actress. Her parents hoped that she would be satisfied with drama opportunities offered in public school and college. Their worse nightmare would be to think that she would entertain the thought of the theatre as a career. They wanted so much more for their daughter.

Their youngest child, Armond, was only ten years old when they moved to Somerville. Out of all the children he was the only one who had a passion for sports. Arianne could not get him to take the least bit of pride in the way he presented himself. When he jumped out of bed in the morning he would rush downstairs to eat his breakfast. As soon as he was finished he did not see any need for something as stupid as brushing his teeth. He just ran for the outdoors. He wanted to see if little Henry had come with his parents Henry and Eliza. Since Armond had never even seen a child with black skin he thought he was the most wonderful friend in the world. He had no idea that there were people in Somerville who would not think kindly of their playing together. This was not acceptable in the south. But that would never stop Armond. He could have cared less about what other people thought. Fortunately for him his parents were not raised with these same prejudices. The Deriveauxs loved the Jones family from the minute they arrived at their villa and found them waiting to greet them. All the Jones family had served them with such love from the beginning. Even though they were employed to do their jobs there was also a genuine friendship.

Armond and little Henry would find all kinds of adventures each day. They loved to play Cowboys and Indians. They would chase each other all over the plantation. Then they would go sit for long periods of time on the bluff overlooking the Mississippi River. As the riverboats and barges would go up and down the Mississippi River, they would talk about the day when they would ride on one of them. Theirs was a friendship that was destined to last a lifetime.

Philippe was filled with love for and pride in each of his children. As he thought about all these things his mind went back to his greatest treasure of all, his beautiful wife. He did not understand all that Charlotte was trying to tell him about Arianne's conversion to Christianity. But he was comforted to know that she was at peace now.

Exhausted from reliving painful memories he closed his eyes and quickly fell asleep. A tug on his shoulder woke him up. He had no idea that he had slept for over an hour. Much to his surprise it was Arienne standing there. "Wake up, sleepy head," she smilingly joked. "Eliza is almost ready to serve dinner. She has prepared a celebration meal for us. We have so much for which to be thankful. I'm anxious to tell you everything. I think we both need to just relish the meal and give thanks to God for the way He has blessed to us."

Philippe escorted his wife to their elegant dining room. All the children had gathered at the table. Arianne made sure that they were all dressed for the occasion. Eliza and her daughters, Mary and Sarah, served the special meal. Mouths watered as they had their plates served with roast duck with fruit stuffing. The stuffing was prepared with seasoned cornbread, butter, grated orange rind, seedless raisins and a large apple. This was one of Eliza's specialties. She had roasted potatoes, glazed sliced carrots, and asparagus spears wrapped in bacon with cheese sauce drizzled over them. Of course, she had made miniature homemade biscuits filled with butter and honey was optional. The dessert was fresh apple cobbler served with whipped cream. Every single member of the family thoroughly enjoyed every morsel. They were praising Eliza. Eliza said, "Why don't we just give a little thanks and praise to God 'cause He's the one who's done made this day a celebration day. He's done set Miss Arianne free." They all bowed their heads and said together, "Thank you, God". This was the first blessing given at the Deriveaux table.

When the kitchen was cleaned to perfection, they waited for James to finish making sure that everything was ready for Mr. Phillipe to start the next day. Then he drove his mother and sisters home in the Deriveaux's truck.

After dinner Arianne was physically drained as was Philippe. It had been a long day but a remarkable one. Indeed it was a day to be remembered in the land to be possessed. This was something she had heard Charlotte say earlier. Philippe escorted his wife to her bedroom and asked if he could help her with anything. With a soft voice she said, "The best thing you could do for me is to share our bed tonight and every night from this day forward." How he had longed to hear those words. It was truly a miraculous day. It was not long ago that his wife had been so despondent that she felt she could not struggle through another day. Now she could not wait to see what her tomorrows would bring. Her only regret was that it had taken so long for her to discover what was missing in her life. Certainly she had every material advantage and the love of her family and friends. She was a gifted artist and had spent many hours trying to find satisfaction in her paintings. As lost as she would get in this passion she would always find that she had to eventually come back to reality. And the reality was that she was completely empty inside. The feeling of guilt for not being able to find happiness in all that she had been blessed with was overwhelming. But today that burden had been lifted. She climbed up onto their tall bed with its beautiful white Battenberg coverlet turned down exposing the eyelet trimmed sheets and pillow cases. They were trimmed with eyelet and blue satin ribbon ran through insertion. The soft down pillows cradled her beautiful face. She curled up into the fetal position and immediately fell asleep.

Philippe went through the house to make sure it was secured. Then he checked on the children and told them goodnight. He returned to their bedroom and snuggled next to the love of his life, his Arianne. All was right with the world now. Sleep was not far behind.

Chapter 7

Although all the Jones family worked in some capacity at the Deriveaux plantation, with the exception of Eliza, Mary, Sarah and James, they seldom saw each other during the day. It was after dark when the women arrived at their modest home. It had none of the elegance of the villa. But it was every inch a *home where love abounded*. Henry greeted his favorite ladies with a big hug and kiss. Eliza never worried about Henry and the boys getting something for supper. As they neared the house they could smell the country sausage that Big John had cooked on an outside fire. Henry scrambled some eggs and made some homemade biscuits. This was their favorite meal. All of them were stuffed.

The evenings in the Jones home were so special to them. After each one took a bath they dressed for bed. Then they gathered in the living room furnished with things that were given to them mostly by the Chandlers. Each one had his opportunity to share things that had happened that day. Needless to say Eliza won the prize for the most amazing story. All of them rejoiced as she told them about Miss Arianne's salvation. Things were certainly going to be different from now on at the Deriveauxs.

Henry suggested that they ought to all just thank and praise the Lord. Everyone agreed. "James, why don't you just sing us a song?" James could sing like an angel and was more than willing at the drop of a hat. He started singing, *"When peace like river, attendeth my way. When sorrow like sea billows roll. Whatever my lot. Thou hast taught me to say, it is well with my soul."* The whole family joined in and filled the house with music that had to have been such a sweet sound in their Lord's ears.

Little Henry, their little budding preacher, opened the Bible and read, *"For God So Loved the World,* (and that be Miss Arianne), *that He Gave His Only Begotten Son,* (and that be Jesus), *That Whosoever,* (and that be me and you and everybody), *Believeth on Him Should Have Everlasting Life* (and that be forever and ever). John 3:16 is the truth. Can I have a witness?" And everyone said, "Amen!"

The family circle was confirmed by holding hands. Henry offered up a prayer of thanksgiving to God for all His blessings to them and for saving Miss Arianne's soul. "Now let's all go get a good night's sleep, 'cause we gonna have another big day tomorrow if the Lord's willing."

Their little wood frame house had only four rooms, two bedrooms, plus the kitchen and living room. They had a well for drawing water and an outhouse. The couch made out into a bed where Big John and Luke slept. James slept on a cot in the same room. Mary and Sarah shared a bedroom. Henry, Eliza and little Henry slept in a bedroom with one bed and a cot. Fresh clean sheets always smelled so good to them. They were washed in a black pot over a fire outside. Then they were wrung out and hung on a line to dry in the sun.

Everything in this house was spotless. It was a family thing where each one did his share toward the upkeep. No one person could have handled this kind of workload.

In the Jones family there was never the sense that they felt sorry for themselves. There was no semblance of envy that the white families seemed to have so much. One thing they knew was that they had been blessed with an abundance of love for each other. Their love for God and their faith in Him had always carried them through the hard times. They knew that He would continue to watch over and care for them. So when they laid their heads on their beds they went into a sound and peaceful sleep.

The sun always came up in the morning to remind them to be thankful that they had the health and strength to do their jobs. They didn't resent being servants. It was honest work. They took pride in doing a good job. The Deriveauxs had not been raised with all the racial prejudices that were prevalent in Mississippi.

Luke and Little Henry remained at home. After picking up around the house they got down to studying. Miss Charlotte had given them beginner math, spelling and reading books but their favorite was the Holy Bible. Luke would read stories to his little brother about little David killing the giant, Goliath, with a sling shot and a smooth rock. He would remind Little Henry that it was really God who gave David the power to do such a thing. They loved stories about Daniel being in the lions' den. Even there God was with him and able to shut the mouths of those hungry lions. After all a lion was only a creation of God. He had no trouble keeping one of his chosen servants, Daniel, safe. After they finished studying, they would climb on an old mare and ride her over to the Deriveaux's plantation. Little Henry looked forward to playing with his special friend, Armond, who was always waiting for him on the front steps.

Many were the days when they would wear themselves out playing in the cotton shed or the hayloft. One day Armond stood in the door of the loft and felt empowered to think he could jump and simply fly to the ground. Little Henry begged him not to do something so foolish. Headstrong Armond just threw his arms out and jumped and flapped as hard as he could. But all that exercise went for nothing. He hit the dirt landing on his back. Fortunately for him the fall was slightly broken as he sideswiped a bale of hay. Little Henry hurried down the ladder from the loft and ran out to see if his friend was okay. Sure enough he lay there still enough to appear dead. "Armond, Armond, is you dead? Don't you go dyin' on me! You wake up, you hear?" shouted Little Henry. Armond blinked his eyes a few times. Slightly dazed he sat up and said, "I can't fly, Little Henry!" After a little rest they made their way over to the bluff overlooking the river. Sitting there they talked about the usual things like the riverboats, barges, and the adventurous river people and future dreams. Neither of them ever mentioned the hayloft fiasco again. Eventually little Henry would get around to telling Armond some of his favorite stories from the Bible. Until that day when that wonderful thing happened to his mother Armond had never heard anyone in his family talk about God or the Bible. Little Henry couldn't believe that there was anyone who didn't know about David and Goliath. This little preacher loved telling his friend all about God's stories.

In the spring of 1924 Celeste graduated from high school. Her graduation gift was a trip to Paris. While there the intense desire to be in the midst of the fashion world became even more of an obsession. She attended every major fashion show. Everyone who was anyone was in attendance. She was glamorous beyond belief. All eyes were focused on her from the minute she entered the show room. With high heels she stood a full six feet tall. Designers wanted to meet her. She was invited to the parties given to celebrate the show's success. Almost every designer offered to help her learn the skills of modeling if she would sign up exclusively with them. It was an overwhelming experience.

Word was sent to Philippe and Arianne in Somerville. It did not take them long to say emphatically that she was to return home immediately. All the arrangements were made for her to attend Mississippi State College for Women in the fall. They would discuss her modeling career after she completed her college education.

Celeste returned after a few weeks with a fabulous new wardrobe. Even the richest students would not be able to compete with her sense of style and her very latest fashions straight from the Paris runways. As disappointed as Celeste was to have to postpone her dream she respected the authority of her parents.

She had few friends in Somerville. This was her own choice. In her thinking most of her schoolmates were unsophisticated. She preferred to spend time with her mother who had an appreciation for the finer things.

While Arianne was depressed Celeste felt her own intense loneliness. She would stay in her mother's bedroom just to be close to her. After Arianne's life changed so drastically instead of feeling great she felt threatened somehow. She had such difficulty expressing her thoughts. She really did not know what was going on in her mind and emotions. All she knew was that her mother was talking about things now that she did not understand at all. When Arianne would say something to Celeste like, "All my life I have thought everything revolved around me and all the people and material things that I needed to make me happy. But I found that this left me unsatisfied and empty. It was not until Jesus came into my life that I was able to see that He is the only One who can truly satisfy my soul and yours." This was the last thing Celeste wanted to hear. She didn't want to live like these "holier than thou" people like the Chandlers and the Joneses did. "Thank you very much but no thanks!" was her reply to such nonsense. This separation between mother and daughter hurt both of them deeply.

The summer seemed to go by in a flash. The time had come for Celeste to leave for her first year at MSCW. Charlotte had recommended "The W" as it was called then. The Deriveauxs wanted their daughter to concentrate on a basic curriculum for at least two years before she started pursuing her modeling career. They knew that she needed a conservative and strict environment before diving into the wild world of godless lifestyles. A trunk and several pieces of designer luggage were packed along with many personal appointments to decorate her room. The Deusenberg was serviced and polished ready to make the drive to the college. Big John was driving and Philippe accompanied his daughter to make sure that she was satisfied with her new accommodations.

Tearful goodbyes were shared by Celeste and her mother and with Edmond, Charles, Vivian and Armand. Of course Eliza was waiting at the car with a basket of her delicious little ham biscuits and some pimento cheese sandwiches. A thermos of lemonade and another thermos of hot coffee were also in the basket. As the car drove away the family waved until it was out of sight. There would be such an empty place without Celeste's cultured influence in the home.

The drive was about one hundred and fifty miles. When they arrived on the campus Philippe escorted his daughter in to meet her housemother. Big John followed with some of her luggage. Celeste had received information about the freshman rules. She had chosen to ignore the part about wearing uniforms. When the housemother saw all the luggage she immediately pointed out this little rule. Celeste told her father that she would rather die than wear those homely things. Philippe calmed her down and assured her that if she would just give it a little time she would adjust. He hated to leave her in this unhappy state but he had to get on his way back to Somerville.

Edmond completed his four years at Ole Miss. He was ready to enter law school now. James drove him to Oxford in Edmond's favorite car, the Erskine. He saw his first one when he went home with his college roommate who lived in Huntsville, Alabama. His friend's father owned an Erskine. Edmond learned that Russell Erskine had designed this amazing car. There were very few of them available. When he returned home he told his father about it. Philippe shared his son's love for beautiful cars. He contacted the dealer in Huntsville and was able to buy one for himself. Edmond was prone to wanting to show off his wealth. He could not wait until he rode onto the campus with this unique car.

Upon arriving at the dormitory, James unloaded the trunk and baggage and took it to his room. All his adoring female friends greeted Edmond. He was indeed a lady's man. Ole Miss had a reputation for being somewhat of a party school. That was perfect for Edmond who had a restless spirit. During the past four years his parents had been notified on several occasions that he was causing a lot of problems with his drinking and sexual exploits. His French accent worked wonders on the girls but created hostility among the boys who were jealous of him. This resulted in arguments that ended in fights. Philippe made restitution where there was damage done. Edmond would apologize and promise never to do that again. His good intentions were often short lived.

Nevertheless, he excelled academically. He never lost sight of his life's goal to eventually go into politics. Every professor encouraged him not to let anything stand in his way.

It was in the first week of classes that he saw a lovely new girl on campus. He thought she was a knockout. Beautiful long blonde hair that looked like shiny silk fell across her shoulders. When she was in the sunlight it looked as though she had turned a light switch on under it. Her complexion was fair and flawless. She had a slight bit of rose on her cheeks. Her eyes were big and blue like the waters of the Greek islands. She was 5 feet, 2 inches tall, and weighed about one hundred pounds. She was perfection and stole Edmond's heart.

There was not a shy bone in his body. He did not suffer from low self-esteem. He ran right up to her and introduced himself. "I am Edmond Deriveaux. Who might you be?" He was the big man on campus. She was a first year student and was impressed that he would notice her. She timidly replied, "I'm Leigh Ann Johnson."

"Is this your first year at Ole Miss, Leigh Ann?"

"Yes it is. And I'll just have to say that it's a bit overwhelming for a little small town girl from Natchez."

"Well, don't you worry about anything. This is my fifth year. I know my way around the school. Let me know anytime you need some help."

They had a little while before each went his separate way, to get to know a little more about each other. Edmond asked if they could meet later perhaps in the dining hall that evening. She agreed and off they went. His heart was racing faster than it ever had before.

Time seemed to stand still as Edmond kept looking at his pocket watch. After attending his classes he returned to his dormitory. Much time was spent getting himself ready for his special date even though it was just dinner in the cafeteria. The anxiety was too much for him. He got there forty minutes before her arrival.

When Leigh Ann walked into the cafeteria, she was a vision of loveliness to Edmond. As many girls as he had wooed and won there was something different about this one. The others were just trophies for show. Leigh Ann was more like a gift to embrace. She wore a light blue chemise that showed off her perfect body and matched her eyes. Her blonde hair was pulled back and tied with a blue satin ribbon.

Edmond jumped out of his chair and ran to meet her. He took her by her arm and they went through the cafeteria line. At the table they did not notice that they had just played with their food. Their eyes were like magnets that wouldn't let go. The conversation seemed to make no sense. They were lost in their immediate infatuation of each other. Edmond appeared more like a neophyte than a suave French playboy.

Finally they shoved their plates away and left the cafeteria. He walked her toward her dormitory. On the way they progressed from holding hands to putting their arms around each other. They stopped to sit on a bench. The moon was full and bright. There was a slight breeze on this fall night. Edmond put his arm around her bare arms and held her close to himself.

"I've never felt quite like this before. I'd be lying if I said that I had not played the field. But I'm feeling things in my heart that make me feel good and scared at the same time. Do you know what I mean?" asked Edmond.

"The same thing is happening to me," said Leigh Ann. "I don't believe in love at first sight but that is exactly what it feels like. Please understand when I tell you that I can't give in to these feelings. We need to get to know each other better. There are so many things I want to know about you."

"I'm not accustomed to waiting for anything. When I feel something and it's this strong I'm used to acting upon it. But I will respect your wishes and do as you say," Edmond answered.

They got up from the bench and slowly walked back to her dorm. Waiting did not mean that they could not kiss. Their lips finally met in a kiss that made both of them know that this would not be their last date. Leigh Ann felt like she was walking a foot off the floor as she went to her room. Edmond ran back to his dorm. Exercise and a shower were the two things he needed desperately.

Due to the difference between their curriculums, one a freshman and the other a first-year law student, their paths did not cross daily. That did not keep them from thinking about the chemistry they experienced the first day they met. Edmond knew that the most important thing in his life was to reach the goals he had set for himself. Nothing was going to deter him from getting that law degree and passing the bar. Then and only then would he be able to think about getting serious enough to zero in on one person with the intention of marriage. For now he had to settle for the things that would temporarily satisfy the lust of his flesh. He had never had a problem finding a pretty girl to meet his needs.

Leigh Ann put a little kink in his immediate plans. It seemed that she wanted more than sex. She had to be sure that she was not a one night stand. It was not that she was a prude. In fact she was going steady with a young man from Natchez. Their relationship had gone as far as you could go without robbing her of her virginity. He wanted her to marry him instead of going off to college. She wanted so much more for herself. Her dreams of a career in public relations were too important to set aside and become a clerk in a store or a secretary. She felt no remorse when she left him with a broken heart knowing that he would never see her again as his girlfriend.

Times were changing for women finally. Susan B. Anthony who had fought against slavery had now devoted her energy to the fight for women's right to vote. Although she did not live to see this fulfilled in her lifetime it did happen in 1920. Doors were opening and Leigh Ann wanted to walk through them.

It was a couple of weeks before she got a call from Edmond.

"Would you like to go with me to a movie on Friday night? I've missed you and would like to see you again."

"That would be lovely. I've missed you, too. What will be playing at the theatre?"

"There's a new Greta Garbo movie, *Flesh and the Devil*, which is supposed to be her best yet. John Gilbert is starring with her. She is such an incredible beauty. You don't even miss hearing her voice in the silent movie," he explained. "I'll pick you up around six o'clock. We'll have a light snack at the coffee house and then make our way to the theatre by seven o'clock."

"I'll be ready and so anxious to see you again. Good-bye until then," Leigh Ann said in a whispery voice.

Leigh Ann felt that Friday night came as slowly as cold molasses poured from a pitcher. The word finally came up from the dorm mother to Leigh Ann, "A young French fellow named Edmond is calling for you."

Leigh Ann hurried down the stairs. There he was more handsome than she had remembered. And to him she was a vision of loveliness. The plans were to eat first and then go to see the movie.

They decided to go to the Coffee House on campus. They served sandwiches including hamburgers and hot dogs, French fries and desserts. Edmond ordered a hamburger with all the trimmings, French fries and coffee. Leigh Ann knew that she was not going to be able to eat much. She was too nervous. She settled for a ham and cheese on rye bread and a coke. Nothing was wrong with Edmond's appetite. His hamburger was gone before she got started.

After finishing their supper they made their way to the only local theatre. When the movie was over they realized that their concentration was not on Greta Garbo but rather on each other. (That probably was a blessing since *Flesh and the Devil* was not the kind of movie two young people with raging hormones should be watching.) His strong arm was around her shoulders most of the time. Sometimes they just held hands. It was like magic the way a simple touch stirred such deep feelings.

The movie ended and they made their way back to Leigh Ann's dorm. They walked as slowly as they could to keep from reaching the door and having to say good-bye. Boys were not allowed beyond the entrance to the dorm.

When they arrived at the door it seemed that time stopped for that little period. They were entranced with each other as though their gaze opened wide the windows of their souls. It could only be called "magic" of some sort. Their lips once again met in a slightly more intense way than the first time they kissed. Not wanting to ever leave this moment they knew that if they were to keep their promise to go slowly they would have to say, "Good-night." And they did.

Leigh Ann went up to her room and fell across her bed. Her roommate was waiting with baited breath to hear about their evening. All that had happened poured out of Leigh Ann's full heart. Edmond was her prince in shining armor. His touch caused her to feel things she had never felt before. She could not wait until she heard from him again. She was sure he was to be the love of her life.

Meanwhile Edmond once again literally ran back to his dorm. His roommate was equally as anxious to get news about the evening. His crude remark was, "Was it a conquest?" Although this was exactly what Edmond would have loved to report normally somehow this infuriated him. "Don't say that about Leigh Ann. She is not like that! I respect her for saying no. We are going to take it slowly. End of subject!"

The weekend was spent with the books. There was much to learn and so little time to study adequately. He had to spend a lot of time in the library. His focus had to shift back to law school. Keeping his thoughts from visions of Leigh Ann and what might have been was the hardest thing he had ever experienced.

Chapter 8

Thomas Middleton thought he was finally on his way to gaining the respect of the Somerville community. He painted his house and married a beautiful young woman. Surely they would think that he was a gentleman and desirable. His egomania didn't fool anyone. They knew he was a tyrant. He tried to put on airs but gave away his true nature when he spent more than thirty minutes with any given person.

Deep down in his heart he could not stand people like Ephraim and Charlotte Chandler. He resented their "perfect little world" with their "perfect little marriage" and their "perfect little children". He could not find anyone in Somerville who had a bad word to say about them. His resentment grew deeper each day. He determined that he would one day show the whole community that he was as important as the Chandlers or any of the rest of that crowd.

Especially annoying to Thomas was Philippe Deriveaux. Behind closed doors he would rant and rave about that foreigner who never had to work hard enough to break a good sweat. Because of Thomas' deprived childhood he hated anyone who he felt had been born with a silver spoon in his mouth. In spite of all his bitterness there was still a driving force within him that wanted to mimic Philippe and Ephraim and try to gain their respect. Thomas' reputation for continued cruelty and neglect where his own children were concerned was public knowledge. The people in Somerville wanted nothing to do with this evil man.

Thomas had envied Philippe since the Deriveauxs moved to Somerville. Every time he saw the shiny Duesenberg with James Jones chauffeuring Philippe or Arianne around he was eaten up with jealousy.

Thomas went to Memphis and bought himself a new Cadillac. Benita went with him and had a short visit with her parents. Thomas told Benita that the first thing he was going to do when he got back to Somerville was to find a colored boy to drive them around town. As they were driving down Levee Road toward their home they saw a good looking young boy walking down the road.

Thomas stopped and asked, "Boy, do you need work?"

"Yes, sir, I sho' do," he replied.

Thomas asked, "Do you know how to drive?"

The young man said, "I been driving since I was fifteen. That's about three years now."

Thomas said, "Come on and get in my new Cadillac. Let me see how good you can handle this big machine. I'm looking for myself a chauffer. You might just get yourself a job today. And by the way, what is your name?"

"My name is Tyrone Wright."

Thomas asked, "Are you from around these parts?"

"No, sir, I was just walking through on my way to Memphis. I been walking since yesterday all the way from Greenville."

Tyrone drove them on to the plantation. It was a great day after all. He had found himself an unexpected job. Thomas finally felt that he had climbed another step up the ladder to social acceptance.

When they arrived home Tyrone was told that he could stay in the little room off the stable. His salary was meager but he had a place to sleep and three meals a day. He would be expected to do other jobs when he was not needed to drive someone. There would of course be no socializing. He was not to forget "his place".

Thomas had one other household servant. Her name was Alice. Her job included housework and cooking. She had a unique personality. Every morning when she reported for duty she could be counted on to tell some wild tale about her family. Since Thomas left early and Benita was left alone. Without any plans for most of her days she welcomed this time with Alice. It was not unusual for Tyrone to come in and join them for breakfast. All three knew that if Thomas returned unexpectedly they would all be in big trouble. Any sign of personal affection for a person of color was unacceptable.

One morning Alice was telling a story about whipping her daughter the night before. She went into a dramatic rendering of the account. She said that when she hit her daughter she would scream, *"Don't hit me, Mama. Our Father which art in heaven. Please don't hit me, Mama. Hallowed be Thy name. Oh, Mama, don't whip me no more. Thy kingdom come, Thy will be done."* This went on until she had finished the Lord's Prayer. Benita and Tyrone were laughing hysterically. Benita said, "Alice, you should go to Hollywood. You are a born actress."

Thomas drove up unexpectedly. He could hear Alice yelling from outside. When the front door opened Tyrone charged out the back door. Alice grabbed the extra dishes, put them in the sink and started washing. Benita sat with her coffee like Miss Astor.

Thomas asked what all the noise was about. Benita made up a story about how Alice was calling for Tyrone to see if he could get free to drive Benita to the beauty shop later in the morning. Fortunately for them Thomas bought their story.

It just so happened that Benita did have an appointment to have her hair bleached. After she got dressed Tyrone drove her to Margaret's Beauty Shop. Margaret was the premier hair stylist in Somerville. She had the best clientele in town. When Benita got there Margaret was working on Charlotte and Arianne. As usual every hair dryer had a lady under it. The two permanent wave machines were working on "natural curly" looking hopefuls. They looked like they were going to electrocute you. Wires came down from a hood like apparatus and clamped a curler on a section of hair. A horrible smell emanated out from the lotion on each curl making everyone feel nauseated. But what could you do when you were born with such straight hair? You prayed through the entire experience that God would keep your hair from frizzing to kingdom come.

Although everyone greeted Benita in a kind way she still felt that they looked down on her from their high pedestals. Margaret had put Arianne's hair into a perfect French twist. Another beauty operator was giving her a manicure. Margaret had pulled Charlotte's dark brown hair back into a bun. Both of these women were as beautiful inside as they were outside. This is what made Benita uncomfortable. She felt as though they could see all the bad things she had thought and done in her whole life. When they talked about Jesus and the church she felt isolated. Thomas would never hear of their going to church.

Like most beauty shops, there were always plenty of women who were more than eager to pass along gossip. Benita felt comfortable listening to people who had problems. It made her feel a bit better about herself. Then Charlotte would find a way to stop the gossip mill by saying something nice about the subject. She never hid her light under a bushel. She used every opportunity to share what Jesus would say about something like gossip and slander. Most of the customers at Margaret's shop were relieved when Charlotte's appointment was on a different day from theirs.

Benita's turn came. Margaret asked her if she would be willing to try a new hairstyle. The famous flapper style would be perfect for her face. Benita thought this was a great idea. The scissors started cutting, hair fell to the floor and the bleach took the natural color completely out. Margaret's hands molded waves across Benita's forehead and on the sides. A curl was formed on each cheekbone. The hair was short in the back close to the neck. Margaret plucked her eyebrows in a dramatic arch and colored them with a dark pencil. Her makeup was strong with blue eye shadow and liner and thick black lashes. Benita loved her new look. Now she could only hope that Thomas would be pleased. Tyrone drove her back home. He told her that she was the most beautiful woman he had ever seen. Benita did not mind his compliment at all. In fact she liked his flirtatious remarks. She knew that she could never let Thomas see her show any kind of attention to a colored man. This did not stop the feelings that were surfacing on the part of Benita and Tyrone.

Chapter 9

The Chandlers had been a big help to the Deriveauxs in deciding on the best college for Edmond and Celeste. Now they were in the midst of getting their own daughter, Daisy, off to Smith College. This institution came highly recommended to them by friends in the northeast. A New England woman, Sophia Smith, received a large inheritance when she was sixty-five. After much deliberation and counsel she wrote this in her will:

"I hereby make the following provisions for the establishment and maintenance of an institution for the higher education of young women, with the design to furnish for my own sex means and facilities for education equal to those which are afforded now in our colleges to young men.

It is my opinion that by the higher and more thorough Christian education of women, what are called their wrongs will be redressed, their wages adjusted, their weight of influence in reforming the evils of society will be greatly increased, as teachers, as writers, as mothers, as members of society, and their power for good will be incalculably enlarged."

Smith College resembled many other old New England colleges in its religious orientation with all education at the college "pervaded by the Spirit of Evangelical Christian Religion but without giving preference to any sect or denomination."

Daisy excelled academically. She was especially interested in their fine arts program. As a young child she dreamed of being a teacher. Her parents had been impressed with her gift for writing her thoughts down in story form or in poetry.

The time came when Ephraim and Charlotte left their younger children with his parents and started out on their long journey to Northampton with their oldest child. There were many planned stops in interesting cities along the way. They arrived at Smith and were pleased to see that Daisy would be living in a "cottage" rather than a dormitory. This was planned to make the student's life more familial than institutional. The housemother welcomed Daisy to their little family. She then told the Chandlers that President William Neilson was expecting them to join the other parents for a reception that evening. It was an encouragement to them to know that their daughter was in such a warm and loving environment. The next day they were able to say good-bye to Daisy and drive back to Somerville with peace in their hearts. Adjusting to her absence would take a little more time.

After another two day drive they were elated over seeing the *Welcome to Mississippi* sign. The family was glad to get them back home. Benjamin, a senior in high school, met them at the car with the good news that he had been elected senior class president. He was an outstanding athlete and had been the quarterback on the Somerville football team since his freshman year. With all his extra curricular activities he did not neglect his studies. As proud as his parents and grandparents were of him for all these things they were even more thankful that he had chosen at an early age to honor Jesus Christ in everything he did. There was no one who ever met him who did not respect him.

Ephraim and Charlotte were anxious to get inside and see the other children. Odeal greeted them at the door and told them that she had a special dinner prepared for them after they had some rest. "Where are the children?" was the first question. "Ruth is in her room with two girlfriends," answered Odeal. (Ruth had started her junior year at Somerville High.) Sam went to the Boy Scout meeting but should be back soon. Sam was a lowly freshman this year but about to reach the Eagle Scout level in the Boy Scouts. That was a real accomplishment for him. This organization had been incorporated in 1910 and chartered by Congress in 1916. Their desire was to build character in young boys through educating and training them to participate in citizenship and to develop personal fitness.

The youngest child, Phoebe, a sixth grader was in her room doing her homework. Odeal started to go and tell the girls that their parents were home but Charlotte stopped her. She wanted to spend a little private time with each of them before dinner. Their children were such special gifts from God. They were never lacking when it came to receiving "*the blessing*" from their parents.

Ephraim and Charlotte had been their children's role models. There is never a guarantee that your children will grow up to be as well adjusted as theirs even when you do the best you can to teach them well. Ephraim and Charlotte had both been raised in godly homes. They had seen the value of living by faith as they grew up. The older they got the more they realized that there was no better lifestyle than the one God can bless.

As each one of his children came to a place in their lives where they knew their personal need to ask Jesus Christ to come into their hearts, Ephaim took them to the family cemetery and told them about his grandfather's faith. He was named after his father. When Grandfather knew that he was going to die he gave some specific instructions to his family concerning his burial. "He was a 'proud old fellow' never wishing to be beholding to anyone in any way. He told the family that upon his death they would have the slaves haul by wagons enough dirt from his own farm to go both under and over his gravesite. He was to be buried standing up so that he would not have to go to the trouble of and take the time to arise when his Savior came back for him on Judgment day. He told them to take bricks made by slaves on his farm to the graveyard to use for his tomb."

Ephraim III carried on his name. He went on to build a prosperous brickyard and continued to live according to the faith of his fathers. He explained to the children that their great grandfather was a little askew theologically. He took this opportunity to share a few truths from the Bible. John 14 told about what Jesus said to His disciples about death. "Let not your heart be troubled; believe in God, believe also in Me. In My Father's house are many dwelling places; if it were not so, I would have told you; for I go to prepare a place for you. And if I go and prepare a place for you, I will come again and receive you to Myself; that where I am, there you may be also. And you know the way where I am going." He then answered Thomas' question about not knowing the way that He spoke of. Jesus said, "I am the way, and the truth, and the life; no one comes to the Father, but through Me." Ephraim explained that when Jesus said that He would come again and receive His own unto Himself; He spoke of the Rapture, which means to be caught up. He went on to tell his son about what Paul shared in I Thessalonians 4:13-18, *"But we do not want you to be uninformed, brethren, about those who are asleep (dead), that you may not grieve, as do the rest who have no hope. For if we believe that Jesus died and rose again, even so God will bring with Him those who have fallen asleep in Jesus. For this we say to you by the word of the Lord, that we, who are alive and remain until the coming of the Lord, shall not precede those who have fallen asleep. For the Lord Himself will descend from heaven with a shout, with the voice of the archangel, and with the trumpet of God; and the dead in Christ shall rise first. Then we who are alive and remain shall be caught up together with them in the clouds to meet the Lord in the air, and thus we shall always be with the Lord. Therefore comfort one another with these words."* It won't matter whether you are buried standing up or lying down. If He tarries all those who have died will go back to dust. The main thing to remember is that when Jesus appears the Rapture of the dead and the living children of God will take place in the twinkling of the eye. This is glorious news for believers. We will see Jesus and be reunited in Heaven with all those we love who have gone before us.

God's blessing was all over the Chandler family. Charlotte, Ruth and her friends, and Phoebe came downstairs. They were anxious to see what Odeal had prepared for dinner. The aroma had filled the entire house. As soon as they sat down to the table, there was a somber moment when they realized Daisy was not in her place. When Ephraim asked the blessing he said a special prayer for Daisy.

Odeal brought the dinner in. She had prepared Ephraim's favorite meal: fried steak, rice and gravy, and fresh green beans. Of course she had made those famous yeast rolls and lemon icebox pie for dessert. He thought he had died and gone to Heaven. The entire family devoured their meal. Ruth's friends asked them if they ate like this all the time. They wanted to move in with the Chandlers.

After dinner they sat together in the living room for awhile. Ephraim and Charlotte told them all about the trip and Smith College. They assured the children that Daisy was going to be very happy in her new environment. Then Benjamin drove Ruth's friends home. The family got ready for bed, said their prayers, and got a much needed good night's sleep.

Chapter 10

When the Deriveauxs decided to make the move from France to Somerville, their dream was to come to this land of promise and plenty and raise their children to have opportunities that would not be afforded them in Europe.

Society and the business world seemed to come apart in the late twenties. World War I had ended in victory for the United States and their allies. But instead of ushering in peace on the home front, there was a concerted movement demanding excesses in lifestyles. The radio and the newspapers and movie newsreels were filled with stories about the infamous flappers. F. Scott and Zelda Fitzgerald were held up as the epitome of free spirits. Scott was hailed as the most gifted writer of that day. Zelda was quoted as saying, "I don't want to be famous. All I want is to be very young always and very irresponsible and to feel that my life is my own to live and be happy and die in my own way to please myself." Everyone seemed to covet an invitation to their lavish parties. Alcoholism took its toll on this out of control couple. It was not unusual for Zelda to dance on tables or dive into fountains. She had to be the center of attention. She sought the attention of men more than anything else. She did whatever she had to do to make sure the cameras caught her doing outrageous things that would surely be on the newsreels. Their lives spun out of control and set the example for many people who envied their notoriety.

Equally notorious was Josephine Baker who was also described as a totally free spirit during this jazz age. She was black, beautiful and very sensual. She performed the "Danse du Sauvage" in Paris where she was given the adulation that eluded her in her own country. When she was in New York to perform in the Ziegfeld Follies, she was not allowed to stay in first class hotels. It was not acceptable for her to touch white people and critics were excessively hard on her. France was her home. Racial prejudice was not an issue there. (This was why the Deriveauxs found it so easy to relate to the Jones family.)

The entertainment world was not the only part of society that had gone crazy. The mafia was on the rise in metropolitan cities like New York and Chicago. It had infiltrated politics to the point that there was not a city, state or national office that was not affected. If there was an honorable man who took a stand against their terrorism, they were often murdered. One such courageous man named Elliot Ness accepted the challenge of going up against this organized crime family. He chose about fifteen men to work with him. They were called the "Untouchables." Their lives were in grave danger each day as Al Capone, the Chicago mafia leader, became obsessed with destroying them. On many occasions Ness barely escaped the car bombs and shootings aimed at his group of brave men.

Ness was successful in bringing Capone to justice. On June 5, 1931, a grand jury returned an indictment against Capone with twenty-two counts of tax evasion. Capone and sixty-eight members of his gang were charged with about 5,000 separate violations of the Volstead Act (This legislature brought prohibition to USA in 1920. The act was introduced by Andrew Volstead, congressman from Minnesota.) The income tax cases took precedence over the Prohibition violations.

Capone was confident that he could get a brief sentence. He pleaded guilty. It was later proven that his gang was bribing and threatening the potential jurors. The judge switched the jury pool with another one that had been assembled for a different trial. They found him guilty of some counts, but not all counts of tax evasion. The judge sentenced Capone for eleven years, $50,000.00 in fines and court costs of another $30,000.00. Bail was denied and Capone was led to the Cook County Jail to wait until he could be taken to Leavenworth.

The government put liens on his property so that they could satisfy its tax claims. The government chose not to prosecute Capone on any of the prohibition violations that Ness and his team had worked so hard to document. The evidence was kept in case Capone was able to beat the income tax conviction. Capone's appeal was denied and in May of 1932, the Untouchables escorted Capone to the train that took him to the Atlanta penitentiary.

Even at this point there was arrogance on Capone's part. He acknowledged that he was on his way to do eleven years but that he wasn't sore at anybody. He said that there was too much overhead in his business paying off all the time and replacing trucks and breweries. He said that the sale of liquor should be made legitimate. Elliot Ness' response to him was that if it were legitimate, he would not want anything to do with it. That was the last time Ness saw Capone.

The Untouchables had done a worthy job for their country. Ness was made Chief Investigator of Prohibition Forces for the entire Chicago division. Syphilis had attacked Capone's mind and body and by the time he almost completed his prison time, the most powerful criminal in America was reduced to a virtual vegetable.

The optimism of the roaring twenties and its "anything goes" philosophy gave way to the pessimism of the thirties. The drastic change started on Tuesday, October 29, 1929, when Wall Street's New York Stock exchange experienced a period of panic in selling of stocks that had never happened before. The Thursday before this the Market had seen a sell off. It was called "Black Thursday." When this was combined with Tuesday's sales it led to a collapse in stock prices and consequently the loss of many American fortunes. The news was replete with reports of investors jumping out of buildings to their deaths. The Great Crash caused people to run to their banks and withdraw their savings causing banks to fail and many hardworking people to lose all their money.

The nation was paralyzed with fear. They had fought and won victories in several wars, but this was the biggest enemy the American people had confronted. The challenge before them was to find their way back to economic health.

Close examination of the causes of the crisis led leaders to see that many people bought stocks with borrowed money and then used these stocks as collateral for buying more stocks. Broker's loans went from under $5 million in mid 1928 to $850 million in 1929. The stock market was unsteady because it was based on borrowed money and false optimism. When investors lost confidence, the stock market collapsed taking them along with it. The economy was not stable. National wealth was not spread evenly. Most money was in the hands of a few families who saved or invested rather than spend their money on American goods. This caused supply to be greater than demand. Prices went up and Americans could not afford anything. Farmers and workers did not profit. Unevenness of prosperity made recovery difficult.

Depression and suicides were the result of lost jobs and money. Pictures were on the newsreels of bread lines for thousands of hungry people. (One man decided that he would see if the Bible was true when it said that God's people would not beg for bread. He reported that as he went down the different bread lines, he asked if each individual was a Christian, and did not find even one.) Poor diets and inadequate medical care caused major health crises. People grew food and ate berries and other wild plants in the country and sold apples and pencils in the city. Landowners planted "relief gardens" for food and to barter.

Living conditions changed as extended families moved into one house. The family members who worked for places like the Telephone Company, Post Office or utilities were able to keep their jobs. Their salary supported other family members without jobs. Divorce went down because couples could not afford separate households. When a woman had to find a job she was blamed for taking the jobs of men.

"Women's work" such as nursing was acceptable. If a woman got an industry job, she was usually paid less than a man doing the same job. Women had struggled for years to get the right to vote. Susan B. Anthony spent her life fighting for the underdog. She fought against slavery and was the first to fight for women's right to vote. She did not live to enjoy that right herself. She died in 1906, before women finally won the vote in 1920.

Somerville did not escape the trauma of these turbulent times. The Deriveauxs were extremely wealthy before they moved from Europe to Mississippi. There security was not threatened as they had a fortune in Swiss banks. Because of this the Jones family's jobs were secure.

Ephraim Chandler understood the importance of only investing what you could afford to lose in the Stock Market. He had inherited a small fortune from his father. Charlotte had her own inheritance that was significant. Ephraim invested in gold, antiques and art. Even though he was the President of the First American Bank, he had been wise enough not to put the bulk of his wealth in an uninsured bank.

Millicent and her children were not affected. They ate what they grew in the fields. Their meat was what Hoss provided when he hunted for deer, rabbit, squirrels and birds. They had fish caught off the banks of the Mississippi and in a nearby catfish pond. They had a cow that gave them their milk. They had lived like this for many years. Nothing changed for them.

There were many Somerville residents who were not as fortunate. One of those was Thomas Middleton. You will recall that he barely survived the poverty in his childhood.

Without an education he determined to become a self-made millionaire before he died. He wasn't "book-smart" but he was "street-smart". He knew enough to listen to people like Ephraim and try to find out how they attained their wealth. He heard just enough about the stock market to make him greedy. He didn't listen long enough to hear how dangerous it was to borrow money that you could not afford to pay back should it become necessary.

On that terrible day when the market crashed, Thomas felt that his life had been destroyed. Indeed his world had collapsed around him because money was his god. He knew that there was not one person who really loved him and would be there for him. The only comfort he could find was in his Jack Daniels bottle.

As the days turned into weeks and weeks into months, he disintegrated into a tormented soul. His mouth spewed out obscenities to everyone in his presence. His violence toward his wife, Benita, got increasingly worse. She thought about leaving him but he told her that he would find her and kill her if she left.

Benita felt some degree of protection knowing that Alice was in the house most of the time and could get Tyrone if Benita needed him.

There were many times when Millicent and the children would hear the screaming and cursing. They did not dare intervene at the house or with the authorities. Thomas was capable of killing anyone who interfered in his life or business.

It did not help that everything Thomas listened to on the radio reminded him that he was a loser. The country had "gone to Hell in a hand basket" and there was no hope for a rescue.

Chapter 11

What had started with entertaining breakfast conversations among Benita, Alice and Tyrone quickly turned into much more. Sensual innuendos between Benita and Tyrone concerned Alice. She knew that no one in Somerville would accept an affair between a married white woman and a black man. The relationship between Thomas and Benita had deteriorated to the place where they were barely civil to one another. One night when Thomas was in a drunken state he went into their bedroom to find his wife. She was asleep. He grabbed her and began to kiss her passionately. To Benita he had turned into a disgusting old man. She wanted nothing to do with him. The smell of liquor on his breath was nauseating. She wiped her mouth and cursed him for touching her. He cursed back and reminded her that he was her husband and he had a right to her body. As hard as she struggled to free herself from his hands she did not have the strength to break loose. He hit her across her face and pushed her down on the bed. Unable to move under the weight of his body he raped her. Thoroughly unfeeling he got up and left his wife crying uncontrollably. He left the house and was gone the rest of the night.

Benita managed to get herself out of the bed and down the stairs. Alice had gone to her home. The only person she could go to for comfort was Tyrone. She went out into the darkness and made her way down to Tyrone's little room by the stables. She knocked on the door. Tyrone opened the door and was shocked to see Benita. Her face was bruised and her eyes were swollen from crying. Weak from her husband's abuse she fell into Tyrone's arms. He picked her up and laid her in his bed. He got a pan of water and a washcloth and wiped her face. He held her until she was able to tell him what had happened. Tyrone was livid but there was nothing that he could do. Fearful that Thomas would come back and find them together he talked Benita into going back to her room. He carried her back into the house and up the stairs and put her gently into her bed. For the first time they gave into their feelings for each other. They kissed and then they both of them cried. The sadness was because they knew that they would never be free to express their love openly. This was forbidden and surely would be punishable by death. Tyrone stayed with Benita just long enough for her to fall asleep. Then he went back to his room. It was the longest night he had ever spent.

The weeks that followed were extremely stressful. Alice knew right away that there was something going on between Benita and Tyrone that was more than just flirting. She warned Tyrone of the consequences of a black man fooling around with a white married woman. But the passion between Benita and Tyrone was unleashed now. They began to find times when they could be together. On drives to the beauty shop or the grocery store or the department store they would find little side roads on the way home where they could park for a little while. Kissing led to other things. As frightened as they were of what would happen if Thomas found out they did not seem to be able to stop their affair.

One day Benita walked down to the barn and found Tyrone rearranging some bales of hay. They kissed and held each other. Then they fell into the loose hay. One thing led to another and they made love. They could not believe that what they felt for each other was as horrible as society said it was. Neither of them made any pretense of being morally pure individuals. They didn't believe in *all this spiritual stuff* so there was no conscience of conviction. As free as they felt with each other they knew very well that if Thomas found out about it one or both of them would be dead. This behavior continued always pushing the envelope barely escaping being discovered.

A month passed and Benita began to feel nauseated when she came down to breakfast. At first she thought that she might have some kind of stomach flu. But it continued and she had to face the fact that she might be pregnant. Her greatest fear was that she did not know who the father was. Was it Thomas as a result of his raping her? Or was it Tyrone? For eight long months she would have to worry about the paternity of her baby. She went to the doctor and he confirmed that she was pregnant. When she got back to the car she told Tyrone that she was going to have a baby. It was a quiet ride back to the plantation.

When Thomas came home that night Benita told him that she had gone to the doctor and found out that she was pregnant. Thomas was elated to discover that he was still able to impregnate his wife. His hard heart did not even remember the circumstances that surrounded the last time he had been with Benita. The relationship between Thomas and Benita did not improve at all. But he went all over Somerville announcing to anyone who would listen that he was going to be a father again.

Eight long months passed. One day Benita was feeling especially tired. Alice insisted that she stay in bed. She fixed her lunch and took it up to her room and found Benita on the floor. She had gotten up to go to the bathroom and her water broke. Benita panicked when she thought she felt the baby's head trying to come out. Alice ran downstairs and out the back door screaming for Tyrone. He rushed up to the house. Alice was talking so fast it was difficult to understand her. He ran up the stairs to Benita. He picked her up and drove her to the doctor's office. Alice went with them. The doctor said we don't have time to get her to the hospital. The doctor confirmed that the baby's head had started to emerge. Benita had to push only two times and the baby was in the doctor's hands. The baby's cry was loud. By every outward sign he was a healthy boy. The look on the doctor's and the nurse's faces were dead giveaways. Something was wrong. When they handed the baby to Benita she saw that he was Tyrone's son. The doctor knew what was going to happen when Thomas found out he was not the father. He insisted that they take Benita and her baby out of his office. She was so weak but Tyrone helped her to the car. Alice wrapped the newborn baby in a blanket and carried him home.

Thomas came home that evening. He had no knowledge of any of the day's events. Alice told him that Benita had the baby and they were in her bedroom. He went upstairs to see his son. Upon discovering that the baby was not white he flew into a rage. He pulled his weak wife out of the bed and beat her unmercifully. Alice knew that he was going to kill them. She ran to the kitchen to find some way to stop him. She grabbed a black iron skillet and ran back up the stairs. Benita was on the floor bleeding profusely. He had kicked her in the stomach cursing her for having carried this black baby in her body. He had taken a pillow and put over the baby's face and held it until the baby stopped breathing. He was going to finish killing Benita when Alice came up behind him and hit him in the back of his head with the iron skillet knocking him out. Alice helped Benita up from the floor into the bed. She then picked up the lifeless baby and put him in his mother's arms. Both women cried hysterically. Benita begged to die.

When they saw that Thomas was coming around Alice took Benita and the dead baby to another room and locked the door. Later Alice came out and looked for Thomas but could not find him. Then she heard a loud noise. She knew it was a gunshot. She ran out the back door and saw Thomas walking toward his truck with a gun in his hand. He got into the truck and drove off. Alice ran to the barn and found Tyrone on the ground bleeding. He had been shot several times. He was dead.

Alice was screaming at the top of her voice. But she had to get back to Benita. "Miss Benita, we gotta get you out of here. Mr. Thomas is gonna come back and he gonna kill you too." She packed some clothes hurriedly and helped Benita get down the stairs to the car. Alice drove just well enough to get Benita to the bus station. She bought a ticket to Memphis. Alice called Benita's parents and told them to meet her at the bus station. She was going to need immediate medical attention. Benita would fill them in on the details later. Alice stayed with Benita until she was on her way out of Somerville. The last thing they talked about was the need to give Benita's baby a name. "Alice, make sure everyone knows my baby's name is Adam. He was my first child and will be my last. I hope God will not hold our sins against him." Alice held Benita and wiped her tears. She assured her that Jesus takes a little baby like Adam into His loving arms and will never allow anyone to hurt him again. Alice said, "Miss Benita, you need to turn to Jesus and let Him heal your heart that's broken all to pieces. God loves you!"

The bus arrived and they heard, "All aboard for Memphis." Benita and Alice hugged. Alice waved until the bus was out of sight.

Alice knew that she had to find someone she could trust to tell all the things that had happened at the Middleton's. Mr. Ephraim Chandler was a good man. He would know what to do. She ran from the bus station to the bank. She told the receptionist that she had to see Mr. Ephraim. It was an emergency. Ephraim heard her raised voice outside his office. He told the receptionist to show Alice in. First he had to calm Alice down. Then he told her to take a deep breath and tell him what had happened. After she told him the whole story he said that they had to go to the police.

In the meantime Thomas had gone to the police station. He told them what had happened. His black driver had defiled his wife and she had his baby. "I shot him," he said with no apparent sense of remorse. The police chief assured him that he would have done the same thing if it had happened to his wife. "Just go get rid of the body. This is justifiable homicide. There's no need for charging you or trying you. You did what you had to do."

Thomas returned home. He drug Tyrone's body to a well and pushed him into it. He then went up stairs and found the cold dead baby. He took the baby to the well and threw him in on top of Tyrone's body. He shoveled dirt in until he could not lift the shovel any longer. Then he took a thick piece of wood and covered the top of the well and nailed it securely. The heartless evil excuse for a man walked away as though he had righted a wrong. He went back to the house. He found it empty. Benita was not there for him to abuse anymore. Thomas had lost everything. He was in such despair that he felt that he had no reason to continue to live. He picked up the gun he had used to shoot Tyrone and sat down at the table in the kitchen. He had a fifth of Jack Daniels to drink until he shut off his tormented mind. At times he would lift the gun to his temple and hold it there. Then he would put it down and drink some more.

Ephraim and Alice went to the police station to report the murders. The police chief told them that Thomas had been there already. He told Ephraim that Thomas was justified in killing that black boy who got his wife pregnant. He was not going to arrest Thomas. Ephraim made it clear that he was leaving but that it would not be the last of the matter.

Ephraim and Alice stopped by and picked up Charlotte. She had such a gift for knowing how to comfort those in need. The three of them drove to the Middleton home. Ephraim suggested that Charlotte go down to Millicent's house and see if they were at home. It was late enough in the afternoon for them to be in from the fields.

Alice took Ephraim to the well. They waited for Charlotte to get back with some others to be with them when they confronted Thomas. They heard a loud shot ring out from the house. They ran to the kitchen door and entered to find Thomas slumped over the table. He had blown his head almost off. The empty Jack Daniels bottle told the story. This tormented soul had no place to turn. He had rejected Millicent's love and her concern for him to turn to Jesus Christ who could have given him the peace that eluded him. He had no compassion for his children. There was no conscience of conviction as he saw them struggle to survive in their poverty. This selfish man wanted only to feed his own egomania. Not one single person really loved him. And quite frankly he did not care. The only part of his face that was still in tact was the eyes. They were wide open with the most frightening appearance of utter fear. It was as though he had been given a glimpse of the judgment of his heartless wasted life. He surely saw Hell as he left this life.

Alice screamed hysterically. She ran frantically from the kitchen. By this time Charlotte had returned with Millicent, Hoss, and Priscilla. Millicent told her daughter Ellen to stay with William and Lawrence. She had always known that things were going to explode one day in that house.

Alice met them, still screaming, "Oh, Miss Charlotte and Miss Millie, Mr. Thomas done shot his head plumb off. And he done shot Tyrone and smothered that little baby and put both of 'em in the well. And he done beat Miss Benita half to death 'cause she done messed up with Tyrone and had a black baby. I done put Miss Benita on a bus back to Memphis. He was gonna kill her just as sure as he killed them others."

Charlotte put her arms around Alice and tried to calm her. Millicent, Hoss and Priscilla ran to the kitchen. Millicent was the only one who had tears to shed for Thomas. Somehow God had given her the grace to forgive him for what he had done to her and her children. No one should have to live a loveless life. But Thomas had not been able to give or to receive this precious gift. Hoss cursed his dead father. His hate ran deep. There was no forgiveness for this man he called a devil. He was glad he was dead. And he was sorry that he had not been there to laugh at him in the face of his agony. Priscilla was not as angry as her brother, but she did not have her mother's ability to forget her own pain.

Ephraim asked Charlotte to drive to the Deriveauxs and get Henry and James to come and help them get the two bodies out of the well so they could give them a proper burial. In the meantime he called the coroner's office and asked for someone to come out and pronounce Thomas dead and take him to the funeral home.

When Henry and James arrived they started the task of getting the dirt out of the well. Hours later they saw the bodies. With a long strong rope they lowered James who was the smallest into the well. He picked up the little baby's body and the men pulled them up. They lowered James again. Exhausted men struggled to lift the weight of two men. The sweat mingled with the tears that were flowing as these strong men were broken by seeing what hate can do to a man's mind.

A graveside service was planned for Thomas. There was nothing a preacher could say that was good and true about him. There was no one who could honestly say that he had done one noble thing in his life. Millicent and all her children, except Hoss, Ephraim and Charlotte, and Philippe and Arianne were the only ones who even bothered to come to the cemetery. No one shed a tear except Millicent and Lawrence.

Henry and Eliza made plans for a funeral service for Tyrone and his son, Adam. They were buried in a black cemetery with a small white cross. On the cross it read, *May They Rest in Peace.* At least they knew for sure that this innocent baby was indeed at peace in the arms of love, Jesus' love. Little Henry read the scripture from John 14. *"Let not your heart be troubled, neither let it be afraid. If you believe in God, believe also in Me. In my Father's house are many mansions. If it were not so I would have told you. I go to prepare a place for you. If I go I will come again and receive you unto Myself that where I am there you will be also."*

James sang, *Swing Low Sweet Chariot, Coming for to Carry Me Home.* There was not a dry eye among the group gathered there. Millicent, her children, the Chandlers, the Deriveauxs, Alice and many others who had heard of this tragedy came to pay their respect. Some might not have sympathized with Tyrone but all of them hurt for the innocent baby.

No one knew about a lone veiled woman who stood in a wooded area and grieved privately. It was Benita. Her parents drove her to Somerville when she heard this tragic news. Her guilt was overwhelming as she knew that her adultery had caused this insanity. If she had just left Thomas when she realized he was incapable of showing any affection to her instead of turning to this vulnerable young man all this might not have happened. She wasn't responsible for the sin sick character of Thomas. She *was* guilty of living a godless life herself. The memory of this day would haunt her for the rest of her life. She got back into her parents' car. They drove home to Memphis in silence. No one but God and her parents knew that Benita was there that day.

Chapter 12

Charlotte invited Millicent, Henry and Eliza to lunch at their house. Of course their children were included in the invitation. There were many issues that had to be dealt with. Ephraim knew that there were legal ramifications dealing with Thomas' property. He was going to meet with the lawyer who had handled Thomas' affairs through the years. The next of kin would be his children. They had to know the financial condition since everyone knew that Thomas was one of the unfortunate ones who had borrowed money to invest in the stock market. When the market fell, he lost almost everything. What would this mean to Millicent and her children? If the house were theirs, how would they pay the taxes since they had been working for a pittance all these years? No one had a paying job. Ephraim would just have to get the facts from the lawyer and then get back with Millicent to advise her.

There was also the matter concerning the police chief. Again Ephraim assured them that he would meet with other civic leaders and deal with this unconscionable miscarriage of justice. Even in a segregated south, good people could not condone the killing of an innocent baby. Henry told

Ephraim that he did not expect to see a change come from the police department. There had always been two kinds of justice: one for whites and one for coloreds.

Odeal announced that lunch was almost ready. Ephraim asked his friends to join him in calling on the Lord for His guidance and help. They all joined hands in a circle of Godly love. A black hand clasped a white hand without hesitation. One thing they knew for sure was that God had given each of them a new heart. He had shown them that He was no respecter of persons. He had created each of them in His image. Each one was special in their own way. They prayed that God would give them the grace and courage to stand firm in their faith as they did what they had to do in the face of deep-seated prejudice. Each one said his own "Amen" and they spontaneously sang, *Bless Be the Tie That Binds Our Hearts in Christian Love.*

They were served on the veranda, where they enjoyed a feast of fried chicken, potato salad, baked beans and a lovely arrangement of fresh fruit. Heavy hearts were made lighter by the acceptance and fellowship given them by the Chandlers.

The Chandlers and the Joneses embraced Millicent and promised her that she was not alone. They would be there for her day or night. Wiping the tears from her eyes, she thanked them from the bottom of her heart. They left with a sense of knowing that they would see something good come out of something evil.

The next morning Ephraim called for an appointment with Robert Matthews, Thomas' lawyer. Robert had all the files pulled when Ephraim arrived. Much to Ephraim's surprise, Thomas had been negligent about revising his will. It revealed that Millicent and their children were the beneficiaries of all that he had. The house and all the land belonged to them now. Even though Thomas had lost several hundred thousand dollars in the stock market crash, he had deeded the house and land to Millicent before the crash. This saved the property. There was still the problem of what Millicent could do about paying the taxes. They had no income.

Ephraim suggested to Robert that they each take one of Millicent's sons under his wing and give him a job starting as an apprentice. If they saw that he was applying himself, they would even see that he got an education. Robert was intrigued by the idea and agreed. He said that their firm, Matthews, Jones and Leeds really needed someone they could train to do some of the research work.

Ephraim and Robert drove out to Millicent's. After talking to her and to her three sons, Hoss, William and Lawrence, they agreed that William would be best suited for the bank environment and Lawrence would be up to the challenge of learning the ins and outs of legal research. Hoss felt like his mother needed him to take care of the plantation. Nothing in him wanted to live in the house his father had contaminated with his evil. He felt that he could never forgive him for the pain he had caused his mother. Ultimately, it was his love for his mother that enabled him to move the family into this comfortable home. She had lived in poverty too long. She deserved to have the conveniences this house offered her. Electric lights and indoor plumbing were things he could never afford to give her. After leaving the Chandler's that day, they spent their first night in the big white house on the hill.

Alice came by the next morning to offer her help in cleaning the house. It was left in disarray after that fatal day. They all got buckets of Lysol water and began the challenge of scrubbing the walls and floors. Hoss took the kitchen where his father had killed himself. It seemed to give him pleasure to see the bloodstains and know that they meant this man he hated was gone forever. He did not hesitate to express his pleasure in knowing that he would rot in Hell forever. This was heartbreaking to Millicent. She knew that if Hoss continued to let this bitterness grow in his spirit, he would destroy his own life. She tried to talk to him many times, but realized that the only thing she could do was to pray for him. And she did just that every day.

When Hoss finished cleaning the kitchen, he said that he would take the mattresses outside to beat them and air them out.

He was in for the surprise of his life. While he was beating the mattress from Thomas' room, he noticed a bit of a tear. He also saw something that looked like a bulge. He ripped the torn place enough to put his hand in and pulled out stacks of bills. He took all of it into the kitchen. He called for his mother and together they counted the money and it added up to five thousand dollars. This was more than enough to pay the tax. There was enough money to buy needed groceries. There was even enough for Millicent to go to the doctor and get the medical care she had neglected.

The family began a careful search through the house to see if Thomas had hidden any more money. They found hidden treasure in other mattresses and in a shoebox under a loose board in the attic. Ellen was given the job of cleaning the musty books. This was not a chore as she had always loved reading. While she was cleaning them, she was thinking about what she wanted to read first. She opened one of the books and found pages cut out and money inserted. Quiet Ellen screamed for her mother to come to the library. They found hundreds of dollars tucked away inside books. By the time they finished, they had to make a trip to the bank to deposit twenty-five thousand dollars.

It just so happened that it was Millicent's 60th birthday. Hoss drove his mother and sisters to Memphis for a day of shopping. All bought new clothes, hats, shoes, purses and they bought suits for William and Lawrence. Hoss did not want anything for himself, but his mother insisted that he had to have something new. He yielded to her insistence and bought himself new khakis and shirts and boots. Oh, and he got a good-looking cowboy hat. They drove back to Somerville in the Cadillac that now belonged to them. For the first time in many years, a figurative window had opened wide showing this dear family that they could indeed have a brighter future. The furrows in Millicent's brow seemed to disappear.

The next day William reported to the bank and Lawrence to the law firm of Matthews and Harrison. Ephraim and Robert agreed that they were a couple of very intelligent and hard working young men. It was a great day when both of them came home with their first paychecks.

Chapter 13

Finally it seemed that things were settling down to a more peaceful pace in Somerville. Ephraim had called a meeting of some of the community leaders to discuss the injustice they had witnessed in the police chief's dealings with the murders. Because of the prejudice against the Negro population, there was a wide difference of opinion as to what should be done. Several men joined Ephraim in making the case for the letter of the law plus the truth that every human being was created by Almighty God and deserves to be treated with dignity and fairness. No one should be looked upon as inferior because of the color of his skin. These were words that challenged everything some the men had been taught all their lives.

The vote was taken at that meeting as to whether they would accept the status quo or whether they would stand together and say that Somerville would be an example to the surrounding communities. They would show that decent, intelligent people could live together in peace. The law would protect all its citizens. No one would have to fear those who were there to keep the peace. The vote was unanimous even though there were a couple of men who reluctantly agreed to give in to this new way of thinking.

Several months later the First Baptist Church had its fall revival. The timing could not have been better. The guest preacher was Dr. Robert G. Lee, pastor of the Bellevue Baptist Church in Memphis. He was one of the greatest speakers in the country, widely respected by people of all denominations.

During that week he preached his most famous sermon, *PAYDAY SOME DAY.*

Millicent had been so troubled by the bitterness and anger that had tormented Hoss. His father was dead but the memories of his cruelty remained. Millicent tried to get him to talk about it with her or with Ephraim. He stoically kept his feelings to himself. She confided these concerns to Ephraim who made it a point to talk to Hoss. He invited him to a men's fish fry before one of the evening services. It was not easy to say no to Ephraim. Everyone had such respect for this Godly man.

Hoss enjoyed the fish and the fellowship of all the men who were there. They were so different from his father. It seemed for that little time, he did not dwell on his painful memories.

After they ate, the men joined the rest of the church. From the minute the organ started playing, Hoss began to feel the strangest kind of sensation in his heart. He was surrounded by people with beautiful smiles on their faces. Everyone welcomed him like he was of such value. It was an overwhelming feeling of acceptance. The acceptance he never had from his father.

Dr. Lee went to the pulpit. He was gifted with the ability to use beautiful flowery phrases. From the minute he started to preach, the congregation was captivated. His text was taken from I Kings 21.

Israel's King Ahab married a pagan wife, Jezebel. To describe Jezebel, he used adjectives such as wicked, daring, reckless, masterful, indomitable, implacable and devout worshiper of Baal. She was the beautiful and malicious adder coiled upon the throne of Israel. King Ahab was described as being the vile human toad who squatted befoulingly on the throne of the nation.

Naboth was a simple man who had a small vineyard close to the palace. Ahab wanted his vineyard for a garden of herbs. He offered Naboth a larger vineyard in exchange for his. Naboth had a sentimental attachment for this property that was his rightful inheritance. He refused to give it up even to the King.

Jezebel took it upon her evil self to take this land for her husband. She wrote a letter and sealed it with the King's seal saying to the elders in Jezreel that Naboth had cursed and blasphemed God. In spite of his innocence he was stoned to death. To most people it looked as though Jezebel was the winner and Naboth the loser. But God spoke through His prophet Elijah that a like fate would befall Ahab.

Many years passed and it looked as though God did not keep His word. Jehu, who had been with Ahab when he went to Naboth's vineyard and declared his desire for it and had seen Naboth stoned, came to Jezreel. Jezebel heard that he was coming and she painted her face and fixed her head and looked out a window. Jehu looked up at the window and said, "Who is on my side?" Two or three eunuchs looked out at him. Then he said, "Throw her down". The men threw her down. Her body hit the street and burst open. Jehu drove his horses and chariot over her. And the Bible says, "And when he (Jehu) was come in he did eat and drink, and said, 'Go, see now this cursed woman and bury her: for she is a king's daughter. And they went to bury her, but they found no more of her than the skull and the feet and the palms of her hands. (II Kings 9:16-26)

Pay Day-Some Day! Even though the mill of God grinds slowly, it grinds to powder. The judgments of God often have heels and travel slowly. But they always have iron hands and crush completely.

At the conclusion of his sermon, Hoss had broken out in a sweat. He had feared that his father had gotten off too easy. He should have been punished severely for all the pain he had caused. Now he knew that God doesn't have a payday at the end of every week. But the payday will come during your lifetime on earth or at the Judgment Seat of Christ. Only the unsaved person will appear before Jesus Christ then. All will be without excuse. They will see all that they have ever done but they will have no opportunity for redemption. Hoss saw clearly that it was up to God to pass judgment on his father.

Dr. Lee made it crystal clear that the Bible says "Today is the day of salvation". He urged the unbeliever to come to Christ, repent of his sins and trust Him for his salvation. Dr. Lee said, "If you will give your life to Jesus Christ, He will make you a new creation with a new heart. You will have eternal life and that life will be abundantly full of peace." Hoss heard all this but he did not know whether God would be able to heal all the hurt in his heart. The scars went so deep. Dr. Lee reminded him again that God creates in a believer not only a new heart but also a new hunger for spiritual things. Old things are passed away, behold, all things become new. While these things fill your heart, God begins the healing process in your soul.

Hoss was really sweating now. The choir began to sing *"Just as I am, without one plea. But that Thy blood was shed for me. And that Thou bidst me come to Thee. O Lamb of God, I come, I come."* Tears streaming down this larger than life size man, Hoss ran down the aisle. He knelt at the altar, sobbing and pleading with God to save his soul. Ephraim joined the pastor and they knelt on either side of this broken man. They prayed with him until God's peace rested on him.

Hoss got up and asked if he could say a few words. You could have heard a pin drop.

"I have lived thirty-two years in pain. God forgive me for the hatred I have carried for my father. I watched other families like the Chandlers and the Joneses and the love they had for each other. It caused more bitterness because I couldn't understand why God would give them all the blessings and not give my mother and us children nothin'. We' been treated like we ain't worth no more than slaves or animals. I've seen my Mama so tired at the end of a day that she just fell out in a faint. I'd pick her up and put her on the bed and I'd bathe her face with cold water. Ever time I'd start ranting and raving about that scoundrel of a father, she would stop me and remind me that it was wrong to act that way. She'd tell me we had to pray to God to help us. I'd yell at my Mama and tell her that God must not know we're down here in this shack, cold or hot, and hungry most all the time. I'd ask her what kind of a God would let that evil man live in that big house while at the same time he was treatin' his "blood" like he was treatin' us. Mama would just say in her soft spoken way, 'Jesus knows our suffering. He was put through more pain than we will ever know. That pain makes Him able to feel ours. God will deliver us one way or another in His own time.' I love my Mama more than anything. But I'd just have to leave when she started talkin' like that. I knew there was no way for us to ever get a break."

"But I've seen God work a miracle when my father's payday came. God lifted us up from poverty and gave us hope for a better life. Now He has shown me a greater miracle than that. He has shown me a way out of my prison of hate. I've asked Jesus Christ to come into my life. I promise Him before you tonight that I will live for Him the rest of my life."

There wasn't a dry eye in the church. Millicent hurried down the aisle to embrace her precious son. Her prayers had been answered. Her other children joined them at the altar. Then the entire congregation moved out of their pews to extend the right hand of fellowship to their new brother in Christ.

The revival continued through the week. Hoss and his family were sitting as close to the front as they could get. It was a new day, a new beginning place with a bright future filled with promise and hope for the Middletons.

Credit goes to Dr. Robert G. Lee's sermon, PAYDAY—SOMEDAY for some of the material from I Kings.

Chapter 14

Four months of MSCW was like a concentration camp to Celeste. It was equally painful for her unfortunate roommate who had realized immediately that she was going to be sharing a room with an elitist snob. Every night Celeste would try on her French couture collection and look at herself in the full length mirror she had brought from home. Then she would hang the clothes back in her closet and put on her pajamas and cry herself to sleep. Her grades were deplorable. She could not concentrate on books when she was so miserable.

Finally the Thanksgiving break arrived. Big John was waiting outside the dormitory to take her home. In her firmest tone, Celeste said, "Big John, pack up all my things. I have *no* plans to return to this ghastly place."

Big John asked, "Miss Celeste, now what yu think yo Mama and Daddy gonna say 'bout this?"

"Don't ask questions. Just do as I tell you! No one is going to make me return to this hell hole. These people can't carry on a sophisticated conversation. I don't think they have any knowledge of European culture. I doubt that they have traveled beyond their Mississippi borders. I am simply bored senseless."

"Now, Miss Celeste, I don't means to be disrespectable but you is sounding like a spoiled chile. Yo Mama and Daddy didn't raise you to look down on peoples. Yu ought to be ashamed of yo self. Now that's jus the way I sees it. But I'm gonna go get yo things and we be on our way," said Big John in an exasperated voice. After a short trip they arrived home.

Much to the disappointment of Philippe and Arianne their oldest daughter repeated her determination to terminate any plans they might have to send her to another college. Celeste declared that she was going to stay at home until after Christmas. Then she was going to New York to fulfill her dream of having a modeling career.

Her parents tried to reason with her and help her to understand that she was too young to be alone in a city like New York. The modeling business was notorious for breeding people who preyed on vulnerable girls. The times were called "the Roaring Twenties" because of the loose morals of many people in the social world. Alcohol flowed freely in spite of Prohibition. Drugs were as much a part of big galas as pate'. "Anything goes" was the password in most segments of society. And if that were not enough there was the real danger of the Mafia influence.

Celeste turned a deaf ear to every word. She was stubborn to a fault. She was absolutely convinced that she was able to take care of herself. She declared that she was going with or without their approval. If she had to she would find a time when she could run away. She knew in her heart that she would have no trouble signing with the best modeling agency in New York. Self-esteem was not a problem for Celeste.

Philippe and Arianne suggested that they table the matter until the next day. What they needed now was to enjoy the dinner Eliza had prepared for Celeste's homecoming. Then they could get a good night's sleep and talk some more in the morning.

When Celeste got ready for bed she went over and sat in a window seat and looked out at the full moon with the sky loaded with stars. She stayed there thinking about the exciting life that was just ahead of her. There was no room for logical thinking about negatives. There was only space in her thoughts for beautiful pictures of her perfect world. Now it was time to fall asleep.

The next day James drove to Oxford to pick up Edmond. Plans had been made for him to bring Leigh Ann home with him for Thanksgiving to meet the family. When they got back to the plantation Armond was the first one to run out to the car to see what this girl looked like. He took one look at Leigh Ann and then ran back into the house yelling, "She's beautiful!" Philippe, Arianne, Celeste, and Vivian went out to welcome her to their home. Edmond took Leigh Ann's hand and said, "Mother and Father, I want you to meet a very special friend, Leigh Ann."

According to their French custom each one kissed her on each of her cheeks. Philippe said, "We are honored to have such a lovely lady in our home. You are welcome here." They all went out and sat on the veranda. It was still warm in Somerville in November. Eliza and her daughters served iced tea with mint and butter cookies. She didn't want them to spoil their appetites. Dinner would be served in a couple of hours. While they were talking beautiful music began to fill the air. Leigh Ann recognized it as being Beethoven and asked who was playing. Arianne told her about their special son, Charles. He was a savant and God had given him this gift. Although Charles could not interact normally with people he could find peace at the piano. There he was able to bless everyone in his home.

After they talked for a while Edmond suggested that he take Leigh Ann for a walk around the grounds. He knew there would be places he could steal a kiss or two. What he didn't know was that Armond was following them. He ran back home ahead of them and reported on every detail of what his brother had done. Philippe reprimanded him for invading his brother's privacy and told him not to say a word about it again.

Leigh Ann was overwhelmed by the opulence in this home. She was from a middle class family. Her father had a good job and made a living that afforded her a college education but it was nothing compared to this. She had seen many beautiful antebellum homes in Natchez. This house was twice the size of any of them. The Deriveaux's had servants, beautiful clothes and jewelry, cars that only a small percentage of people in the country could afford. All this affluence had not made them snobs (with the exception of Celeste maybe). Leigh Ann shared Celeste's bedroom while she was visiting. They had very little in common. Before the weekend was over they grew to understand each other enough to be friends.

Morning came and the family woke up to the smell of turkeys roasting in the oven. It was Thanksgiving and Eliza, Sarah and Mary were busy preparing a feast. Eliza took time out to make homemade sausage and biscuits and cinnamon rolls for breakfast.

Then she got back to her baking. There were pecan pies and pumpkin pies for dessert. Sweet potatoes were peeled to make a fluffy casserole. Of course the turkey called for southern cornbread dressing and giblet gravy. Cranberry sauce, green beans with new potatoes and beets completed the meal. Every member of the family thought they would die before they got to eat. The aroma let them know that this was a Thanksgiving meal to die for.

Finally they were seated at the massive table. The centerpiece was an attractive cornucopia created by the local florist. Philippe drew attention to this and pointed out how God had blessed their family since they had moved to Somerville. Although he had not yet made his personal profession of faith in Jesus Christ as Arianne had he still asked them to bow their heads so they could give thanks to God.

"Almighty God, we give You thanks for all Your blessings. Amen."

The Deriveauxs devoured the meal. Somehow they managed to enjoy both kinds of pie with coffee. Then they made their way to the parlor. There they were entertained again by the amazing music that came from Charles.

Chapter 15

The word got around Somerville in a hurry that some of the community leaders were out to get colored people fair treatment under the law. As far as some local people were concerned things were fine as they had always been. Their view of the coloreds was that they liked their life the way it was. No matter what the likes of Ephraim Chandler thought there was not going to be any giving in and mixing of the races. They were infuriated that the Chandler's had allowed the Joneses to eat at their table.

A group of bigoted men got together for their own meeting. It didn't take long for them to feed on each other's hatred and fears. They made plans to talk to some men in a neighboring town who were members of the Ku Klux Klan. The KKK was always ready to robe up and terrorize innocent people who happened to be black or Jewish.

They waited about a week before putting their plan into action. Late one night they loaded up in several pick-up trucks and headed for Somerville. Their target was Henry Jones' house.

Henry, Eliza and their children were sound asleep. So much had been happening. They were exhausted. They were awakened by the sound of something crashing through their window. They jumped out of bed and hurriedly put on some clothes and went into the living room where they found a rock with a note tied to it. The note read, "You are going to die if you don't quit trying to act like you are white." Henry put the note in his pocket so that he could keep the children from seeing this ignorant garbage.

Henry looked out the window and there in his yard stood a burning cross. The cowards hiding behind their hoods hurriedly jumped on the backs of the pick-up trucks and drove off. One truck made a turn around the house and one of the men threw a fiery torch onto the back porch of the house. While the Joneses were looking at the horrible sight in the front the back of the house was set ablaze. The old wood frame house went up in flames like it was a cardboard box. There was no way to draw water to put it out. The most important thing was to get the children out where they would be safe. Each one grabbed something on their way. James got his guitar. Sarah gathered up as many clothes as she could hold. Eliza thought to call the telephone operator before the fire burned the line. She told the operator to call the Deriveauxs, the Chandlers and Millicent and tell them their house was burning to the ground. She got the message across before the line went dead. Luke was gasping for breath because of his asthma. He managed to carry out the old box of family pictures. Mary's temper flared and in her anger she grabbed the shotgun and rifle Henry and Big John used when hunting for deer and rabbits. She very well intended to use then if any of these hooded hoodlums were hanging around to enjoy the show. Little Henry saved the family Bible. This was the most precious thing in the house to him. Henry and Big John carried a few pieces of furniture out. Eliza went in to try and help but was overcome by the smoke and passed out. Big John picked her up like she was a baby and carried her to safety. The girls gathered a bucket of water and bathed her face until she came around.

Hoss was sitting out on his porch that night. He saw the trucks filled with KKK members. They were shouting and cursing and drinking beer like a bunch of crazed maniacs. Hoss looked in the direction they were coming from fearing that they had burned a cross on someone's yard. He saw the fire and knew that it was the Jones' house that was burning. He went in to wake up his mother. She told him that the operator had just called and told her about the fire. They woke up the other children and went down to help.

It wasn't long before the Deriveauxs and the Chandlers arrived. No one could believe that anyone would do such a dastardly thing. Henry assured them that this was the way things had always been and the way they would always be. "Nothin's ever gonna change for us 'til Jesus comes to take us home with Him," Henry said matter of factly.

Their house and virtually everything they owned were destroyed. But they praised God that everyone was alive. God had sent them all these caring people to comfort them. Immediately Charlotte had a plan for housing them. The Deriveauxs would take Henry, Eliza, Big John and Little Henry to their home. Edmond and Celeste were gone now and their rooms were empty. Millicent asked that James and Luke come to stay with them. Charlotte put her arms around Mary and Sarah and took them home with her. Tomorrow they would get together to make plans for the immediate needs and the future needs. Henry and Eliza hugged and kissed each of their children and promised them that God would see them through this trial. He took the Bible from Little Henry and opened it to the fourth chapter of Philippians, and he read *"My God shall supply all your needs according to His riches in Glory by Christ Jesus."* "Now, children, that don't mean *some* of our needs. That means *all* our needs." They left the ashes and kept their focus on the things that matter the most, God, family and friends.

There were three households in Somerville that did not get much sleep the night of the fire, the Deriveauxs, the Chandlers and the Middletons. In the morning Ephraim went to his office and started making phone calls. He summoned some of the key city leaders together to decide what they could do for the Joneses. There was not a man among them who did not agree that this was an outrage. Everyone respected Henry Jones. He was an honest, hard working, and honorable man. One by one they contributed ideas as to how to help this family.

Phillip Deriveaux spoke up first and said that he would provide the financial assistance needed to build them a new house. Ben Harris, owner of a building and supply company quickly added that he would let them have the building supplies needed for cost. Larry Brown was an electrician and owned an electrical supply business. He made the same offer as Ben, supplies at cost, and he and some of his men would wire the house. He said he knew that Joe Burris would be glad to join in and roof the house with the same deal at cost. Ephraim picked up the telephone and asked the operator to call Edgar Watson, the local plumber, for him. When Edgar answered Ephraim explained the situation. Everyone was relieved to hear Ephraim say, "God bless you, Edgar, I knew you would want to be a part of this work of kindness. Everyone was on the same page when it came to the starting date. "As soon as possible" was the only response. The men put on their work clothes and got together with the Jones men and Hoss and began the task of clearing off the burned remains. A neighbor brought his tractor over and leveled off the ground. Within a few days work had started to lay the foundation for their new house.

At the next prayer meeting at First Baptist Church they presented the needs of the Jones family to the members. One after another stood up to offer help. One man said that he had a small rental house the family could live in rent free until the house was completed. The owner of a furniture store said that he would give them mattresses and box springs. Some of the women offered quilts they had made. Clothes were provided by several local merchants. Department stores gave them pots, pans, dishes and flatware. It was one of the best evenings this church had experienced. It was a time of giving sacrificially. They remembered that Jesus had said that if you do it unto the least of these you do it unto Him. The word got out into the larger community. Offers came in from everywhere. Every need was met. The people worked as one on the house. Three months later it was completed. A beautiful new wood framed house. They agreed that they would paint it yellow and white. The yellow was because it was as full of life as the sun. And white because it was built out of pure undefiled gifts of love.

The house had a living room, three bedrooms, an indoor bathroom, a kitchen and a dining room. There was indoor plumbing and electricity. There was a porch on the front of the house and a smaller porch on the back. It was a dream come true for this dear family.

The KKK had done its best to destroy good people through an act of hatred. But God moved in the hearts of His people to restore them through acts of love. Somerville became a better place to live that summer.

There was a big housewarming when the day came for the big move. Everyone helped in his own way. Odeal, Ella, Alice and Eliza joined together to prepare food for the crowd. There was fried chicken, potato salad, baked beans, corn on the cob, apple turnovers, Odeal's homemade rolls, watermelon and tubs of cold drinks. It was a victory celebration. Laughter and music filled the air. Praise was offered up to God who was the One who had moved in the hearts of His people to make this occasion possible.

Chapter 16

Several years had passed since that black Thursday that paralyzed most of the United States. The great depression had destroyed the wealth of many. Hope came when Franklin Delano Roosevelt was elected president in 1933. His appearance, though he tried to hide his disability, was not that of a physically strong leader. He had polio and at that time it was crippling. The vaccine would be developed in the fifties. When he spoke to the nation over the radio, the listener never thought about the fact that he was in a wheelchair. He told the nation that with the help of many others, he had come up with programs to help those who were helpless to help themselves. He called it "New Deal" programs. He feverishly created programs to give relief, create jobs, and stimulate economic recovery for the U.S. These programs were call "Alphabet Soup" as well as the "New Deal". The compassion in his voice made him believable to almost everyone.

Immediately he shut down all the banks in the nation and forced Congress to pass the Emergency Banking Act which gave the government the opportunity to inspect the health of all banks. The Federal Deposit Insurance

Corporation (FDIC) was formed by Congress to insure deposits up to $5,000.00 dollars. This restored the people's faith in banks. Government inspectors found that most banks were healthy and two-thirds were allowed to open soon after. After reopening, deposits exceeded withdrawals.

The Federal Emergency Relief Administration made available to local relief agencies $5 million. This program also funded public works programs. The belief was that men should be put to work and not given charity.

The Civilian Conservation Corps (CCC) and environmental program put 2.5 million unmarried men to work maintaining and restoring forests, beaches and parks. Workers earned only $1.00 a day but received free board and job training. From 1934-1937 this program funded similar programs for 8,500 women.

The Indian Reorganization Act of 1934 ended the sale of tribal lands and restored ownership of unallocated lands to Native American groups.

The Federal Securities Act/Securities and Exchange Commission (SEC) required full disclosure of information on stocks being sold. The SEC regulated the stock market. Congress also gave the Federal Reserve Board the power to regulate the purchase of stock on margin. This was not pleasing for businesses.

The Home Owners Loan Corporation (HOLC) helped people keep their houses. They refinanced mortgages of middle-income homeowners.

The Tennessee Valley Authority (TVA) helped farmers and created jobs in one of America's least modernized areas. This reactivated a hydroelectric power plant and provided cheap power, flood control, and recreational opportunities to the entire Tennessee River valley.

The Works Progress Administration (WPA) was an agency that provided work for eight million Americans. The WPA constructed or repaired schools, hospitals, airfields and many more projects.

The Farm Security Administration (FSA) loaned more than $1 billion dollars to farmers and set up camps for migrant workers.

The National Labor Relations Act legalized practices allowed only unevenly in the past such as closed shops in which only union members can work and collective bargain. The act also set up the National Labor Relations Board (NLRB) to enforce its provisions.

The Fair Labor Standards Act banned child labor and set a minimum wage.

The Social Security Act established a system that provided old-age pensions for workers, survivor's benefits for victims of industrial accidents, unemployment insurance, and aid for dependant mothers and children, the blind and physically disabled.

These and many other things credited to FDR brought the American people and the economy out of this dark period called The Great Depression.

FDR's wife, Eleanor, was one of the most respected women in history. During her husband's presidency she changed the role of First Lady from hostess to human rights activist. She fought for the rights of women and African-Americans and against poverty and child labor. She took over many of her husband's duties because he was crippled by polio.

The country was divided when it came to acceptance of Eleanor's fierce independence. Many criticized her for traveling across the country and abroad when she had children who needed their mother at home. Her husband was under enormous pressure trying to get the economy back on track. Certainly he needed his wife by his side during these difficult times. None of the criticism bothered her since she felt that she had a mission of her own. She would not allow anyone to hinder her from accomplishing her task.

The people who loved her the most were the underdogs who needed to have someone champion their causes. What better activist could they have than the First Lady of the United States?

President Roosevelt was immensely popular. His approval rating continued to climb as thousands of people found jobs. It was not long before the most popular song in the country was "Happy Days Are Here Again".

Somerville was no exception to the rule when it came to benefiting from the New Deal programs. Ephraim's bank started to thrive again. People felt comfortable putting their money back into savings accounts.

Jobs were available for men and women who were ready and willing to work. Loans were available to those who wanted to buy a house or start a small business. The future looked brighter than it had for such a long time.

Chapter 17

After Thomas Middleton died Millicent and her children moved from the shanty to the big house on the hill. This was quite an adjustment for a family who had known humiliation and poverty. It was wonderful not to have to go to an outhouse or to draw water from a well. Sometimes they felt as though they were inside a dream and would wake up soon to find out that they still lived in the dilapidated dwelling. They kept reminding each other that they would never have to endure the cold that came through the cracks in the walls in the winter. No more buckets would have to be placed strategically to catch the water when it rained.

Each new day would find them gathered together praising God for their deliverance. Millicent had been faithful when it came to teaching her children the truths of the Bible. By the light of a coal oil lamp she read God's Word each night. She prayed for each one of her children daily. Most important of all was the example she set for them in the way she lived a Godly life. She never belittled her children's father to them. She would scold Hoss when he lashed out against Thomas. Her heart was pure and her countenance reflected the radiance of Jesus Christ in the midst of her poverty and physical weakness. The only thing that changed when they inherited the material wealth as a result of Thomas' death was that she could now see that her children would have an opportunity to achieve their individual goals. No longer would they be fenced in to a lifetime of poverty. She continually praised God for such a blessing.

Hoss was doing an excellent job managing the plantation. He found some strong young men to work the fields. They planted cotton and the first year they gathered the greatest yield ever. Everything seemed to be particularly blessed. The sheep multiplied at a rapid pace. The market was ready for the wool and cotton since the economy was improved. The plantation realized an amazing profit the first year.

William was perfectly suited for the bank. Ephraim took time to personally teach him the ins and outs of the business. Plans were made to enter William in Memphis State after the first year. He needed to get a business degree. Ephraim could see his potential. It would not take long before he would be ready for a position in management. His future looked bright.

Lawrence loved the work at the law firm. He was fascinated by the research. Digging into old records and searching through newspapers for information needed to build a case for the lawyers was like an adrenalin rush. Everyone knew that he would go on to become one of Somerville's great legal minds. He might even find himself on the Supreme Court one day. Lawrence was always a dreamer and his dreams were huge.

Priscilla continued to find her pleasure in her love for running. One day she was flying down Levee Road unaware that anyone was observing her. Billy Curtis, the head track coach at the University of Tennessee was visiting his grandmother in Somerville. They were sitting in the swing on her front porch talking about old times. When he saw Priscilla's running style, the grand stride of a graceful gazelle, he knew she was the discovery of a lifetime.

"Granny, who was that?" he asked.

"Why that was Priscilla Middleton," she replied. "She runs by here everyday rain or shine. Why did you ask?"

"Granny, can you introduce me to her? I've got to meet her. I've got to convince her to let me be her trainer. This girl could go to the Olympics one day. I'll bet money on that."

Granny Rose went right inside and asked the operator to ring 484, please. Millicent answered. Rose asked if her grandson could come over and meet Priscilla. She explained that he was a track coach at UT and was captivated by Priscilla's style of running. Millicent invited them to come over that afternoon.

When Billy and his grandmother arrived, Priscilla met them at the door. She was intrigued by this stranger who was asking about her. They sat down in the living room. Millie had the coffee service ready. After a cup of coffee, homemade chocolate chip cookies, and small talk they got down to the business at hand.

Billy addressed Priscilla, "How long have you been running?"

"Ever since I can remember," answered Priscilla.

"Have you ever done any track and field training?" Billy asked.

"No. I haven't been able to spend the time necessary to practice with a school program. My family has had to work in the fields most of my life and that didn't leave much time for school activities. I just ran late at night most of the time. Now that I don't have to work in the fields I can spend more time running. I feel like I'm totally free when I'm running. Sometimes I don't realize that I've run as much as twenty miles. But I'm not all that tired. In fact the longer I run the more energized I am."

Billy said, "Priscilla, you have a God given gift. It would be a shame not to use this gift in competitive sports. I believe that with the right training you could eventually go to the Olympic Games. I would love to have the privilege of training you in the UT sports program. I can get you a full athletic scholarship. You can get a great education plus fulfill your potential for greatness in your sport."

"I don't know," Priscilla answered. "Mama needs us here. She's not in good health."

Millie jumped in and assured her daughter that she must not turn down this incredible opportunity. "All you children have worked tirelessly and have had no chance to realize your dreams. Well things have changed around here. God has delivered us out of our poverty. My health is not an issue here. I am able to get good medical care now. I don't have to work when I'm sick. I am getting stronger everyday. My precious child, I want you to have the opportunity to fly as high as an eagle. Say yes to this kind man."

A smile broke out across Billy's face. In his heart he whispered a little prayer, "Please, God, let her say yes." Priscilla put her arms around her mother and hugged her tightly. "I love you, Mama. I will accept Mr. Curtis' offer. If I have any success I will tell everyone that it was my Mama who taught me to discipline myself and settle for nothing but God's best in my life. Even when I wanted to run away from all the injustice our family endured because of my father I knew the most secure place I could find was at home with my devoted mother. We were poor in the physical sense but rich in what counts. Mama showed us how to love one another and have to trust God for all our needs." Tears streamed down Millie's face. In fact Granny Rose and Billy had some moisture in their eyes too.

Billy told Priscilla that he was returning to Knoxville the next day. There was time for him to put everything in motion in order to get her ready for entrance into UT in the fall. Billy and Granny Rose left. Priscilla's emotions were mixed. She woke up that morning expecting another regular day. She ended the day with anticipation of a whole new world opening up to her. Millie and Priscilla immediately started making plans about what she would need for her college wardrobe.

When the family gathered for dinner Priscilla took great joy in sharing her good news. Everyone was excited for her. The first thing Hoss thought about was free tickets to UT sports events. Melanie had a vision of visiting her sister in her dormitory and meeting college boys. Ellen was as happy as the others but had no desire to leave her protected and private environment. Interacting with strangers was her worse nightmare. William and Lawrence were so caught up in their new career challenges there was not room for thinking about anything else.

The summer would seem to go on forever. But the knowledge that her dreams were going to be fulfilled beyond her wildest imaginings kept Priscilla going. Each day she found that she had extra strength to run even extra miles. Coach Billy had compared her to a gazelle running with elegant grace. For the first time in her life she felt that beauty in her soul. It seemed that she did not even touch the ground but rather like she was gliding above Levee Road. Running had always been her passion. Now it was filled with the promise of an amazing future.

The years of struggle and poverty had hindered Millicent from seeing Ellen's inner pain. Ellen was her second child. Her temperament was introverted and melancholy. She lived in the shadow of her older brother, Hoss. His explosive tirades against his father frightened Ellen. As she grew up and learned to read she retreated into books. When she was not working in the field you could find her in a quiet place reading. Millicent was preoccupied with her family's survival and dismissed Ellen's behavior as "*just the way she was*".

After they received the inheritance from Thomas Millicent was able to devote more individual time to her children. One day she knocked on Ellen's bedroom door. Ellen told her to come in. Millicent found her daughter sitting at a desk. There was a stack of papers beside her. She inquired as to what she was writing. Ellen told her that she was trying to write a novel.

"Mama, I have all this stuff in my head and I didn't know what to do with it."

Millicent asked, "What kind of things are you thinking about?"

"Mama, I'm writing down my feelings that I've had for all these years. I struggle with why our family had to live in such poverty. I think about Daddy and why he didn't love us. There are so many other things I've never felt free to talk about. I feel like if I don't get it out I'm going to go crazy. I don't know how to talk about this to you or anyone else but I think I can write it down."

Millicent reached down and put her arms around her. "My sweet baby, I've neglected being there for you. I never knew that you were hurting. I thought you just preferred to be in your little corner. Please forgive me. You have always loved to read. I am certain you will know how to write your thoughts down. Will you please let me read these pages when you feel free to share them? Just think, Priscilla is going to the Olympics one day according to Coach Billy. And I just bet you that you will have a book on the bestseller list one day. I am so proud of you. I love you more than you will ever know. Now I'm going to go and let you get on with your work."

Opening up to her mother was therapeutic for Ellen. She picked up her pencil and continued to write from her heart.

As Millicent started down the hall she stopped and looked into Melanie's room. Melanie was her youngest child. The whole family had protected her from as much of the ugliness as possible. She was petite with porcelain skin and blonde hair. Her older siblings had always treated her like she was a precious doll.

Unlike Priscilla, the athlete, and Ellen, the bookworm, Melanie was obsessed with her femininity. She loved to *dress up* and play with her dolls. Her mother made most of them but that didn't matter to Melanie. She was born to live the life of a diva. Spoiled was the best way to describe her. Somehow no one seemed to resent her. She was a ballerina one day and an actress the next. Each one of Millicent's children was uniquely different. To have known such poverty and rejection it was a miracle that they were as well adjusted as they were.

The family's new lifestyle afforded them the luxury of going to a movie at least once a week. A beautiful little actress whose name was Shelly Grant captivated Melanie. She was soon referred to as America's "little sweetheart." A tiny starlet with loose curls and a smile with dimples in her cheeks that melted your heart, that was Shelly. She could sing and dance and act with a talent that amazed the movie industry. She often played an urchin or poor little girl but she always got her way with wit and charm.

Shelly was performing from the age of three. Her father was a banker. A convention of bankers met in Los Angeles, California, one year. Ephraim and Charlotte took their daughter, Phoebe, and her best friend Melanie with them. While Ephraim attended the meetings he met Shelly's father. He told him how much his daughter and her friend loved Shelly. Mr. Grant asked him if his family would like to come to their home for dinner one night. Of course he readily accepted. When he told the girls, they screamed and danced around the hotel room like they had won the lottery. They could not wait for the hour to come for them to leave.

Finally they stood at the entrance of Shelly Grant's home. Even though they were quite a number of years older it didn't matter to them because they simply looked at her as an icon. Much to their surprise Shelly opened the door.

She looked exactly like she appeared on the movie screen. With that twinkle in her eye she invited these strangers into her home. It was no wonder this precocious doll like child had become the bright little spot in the Depression years of the 1930's.

When the evening came to an end it was hard for Phoebe and Melanie to turn loose of being in Shelly's presence. Much to their surprise Shelly suggested that they be pen pals.

When they returned to Somerville Phoebe and Melanie wasted no time in calling all their friends to tell them about their wonderful experience. From that day forward both girls dreamed of one day becoming actresses. They put together all kinds of acts and sold tickets to family members. To everyone's surprise there seemed to definitely be a couple of fairly talented young ingénues.

During these years of economic revival movies and comedians were a source of great pleasure. Joy had been missing in the midst of the tribulation. They hungered for a reason to smile and laugh again. People enjoyed the dramatic movies as well as westerns and most of all the musical extravaganzas.

Clark Gable was one of the most talked about actors. His suave, debonair looks and that husky voice won every woman's heart. He was the leading man to beautiful women like Carole Lombard and Claudette Colbert. Fred Astaire danced his way into your life and Bob Hope, with his ski nose and sharp one-liners, kept you in stitches.

The levity was often interrupted by the newsreels sometimes with good news but more often with bad news. In 1933 there was always something about President Roosevelt.

The ground breaking for the Golden Gate Bridge in San Francisco was of great interest to the entire country. How were they going to accomplish such a feat? Prohibition was over and that gave way to much arguing about the pros and cons. No one at the time knew the importance of the announcement that Adolph Hitler became the German Chancellor.

The FM radio was invented and that gave each home a way to keep up with national and international news. Sitting around a radio was treasured time for families. There were radio programs like "Inner Sanctum", a terrifying thirty-minute script. The sound effects were so eerie that children and adults would not be able to go to sleep. There were some hysterically funny programs that cheered you up after being scared witless.

Each aspect of the entertainment industry appealed to Phoebe and Melanie. Their families prayed that at some point they might get this out of their systems. No parent wanted his or her little girl to go to Hollywood.

Chapter 18

A few weeks had passed since Celeste hastily moved to New York. Philippe had made sure that she was settled in an apartment in a safe area of the city. The Huntington Modeling Agency saw her potential and did not waste any time signing her. They assured Philippe that they were protective of all the young models in their agency.

Philippe returned to Somerville and told the family all the details. He felt confident that Celeste was mature enough to handle living on her own. After all she had been raised in Paris. It was not like a little country girl from Mississippi overwhelmed by the hustle and bustle of the big city.

Nevertheless the Deriveaux home experienced the emptiness that came from one of their little birds leaving the nest. Edmond was in his second year of law school. Vivian was a senior in high school. She was an exceptional student. Benjamin Chandler occupied a great deal of her time. What had started out to be a comfortable friendship had developed into a sincere love. Everyone thought they were too young to know what true love was but there was no doubt in these two young people's hearts about its reality. Benjamin was the most outstanding athlete at Somerville High. His record as quarterback of the football team impressed many universities. The amazing thing was that when he finished the football season he was ready to take his position as a forward on the basketball team. As if that were not enough he excelled in the spring as the ace home run hitter on the baseball team. There were three different options for him as far as athletic scholarships were concerned. Vivian did not miss a game. She was his loudest cheerleader. The family seemed to see less and less of Vivian.

The Deriveaux mansion seemed to get lonelier with each passing year. Of course Armond was just in the eighth grade. He and little Henry were still best friends. Although they did not go to the same school and the level of education differed in the segregated schools Armond shared everything he learned with Little Henry. Little Henry shared the thing he knew best with his friend. He shared the teachings of the Bible.

Armond had seen the difference in his mother's life after she invited Jesus Christ to come into her life. But he didn't understand all the things that pertained to faith. How can you believe what you can't see? It just did not make sense to him. One day when he and Little Henry were sitting on the bluff watching the boats go up and down the river Little Henry told him about a man who was a tightrope walker.

The man said to a crowd of people gathered at Niagara Falls, "Do you think I can walk across the falls on this tightrope?"

The people said, "Yes."

The man took his balancing pole and walked across without any problem.

131

The man asked, "Do you think I can go back across pushing a wheelbarrow?"

The people enthusiastically said, "Yes."

He took his wheelbarrow and carefully pushed it across the tightrope. There was thunderous applause.

He said, "You have seen what I can do. Now will anyone get in the wheelbarrow and trust me to push you across the tightrope to the other side of the falls?"

There was dead silence. No one responded. Finally one voice spoke up. "I will get in the wheelbarrow."

He got in and was pushed safely across to the other side. The people applauded and yelled to the top of their voices.

Little Henry said to Armond, "My friend, that's what faith is. Think about it like Jesus has a wheelbarrow and is asking you to get in it and trust Him to get you to Heaven. It is trusting with your life as well as believing in your heart that Jesus Christ is who He says He is, the Son of God. You believe that Jesus can do what He says He will do and that is save your soul. He shed His pure untainted blood on a cruel cross so that blood could cleanse you from all your sin if you will only trust Him. Romans 10:9-10, says, *"If you confess with your mouth that Jesus is lord, and believe (trust) in your heart that God has raised Him from the dead, thou shalt be saved, for with the heart man believes (trusts) unto righteousness and with the mouth confession is made unto salvation. And in verse 13, it says for whosoever calls upon the name of the lord shall be saved."*

The Holy Spirit opened this truth up to Armond. He was convicted in his heart of his need for God to forgive him of his sin. He wanted desperately for Jesus to come into his heart. He wanted to live for Jesus just like his best friend,

Little Henry. Best friends became spiritual brothers in an instant. There was great rejoicing in the Deriveaux home that day as the boys shared their good news with Philippe and Arianne as well as Henry and Eliza. Now two members of the Deriveaux family were heaven bound. Prayers would continue to go up for the rest of the family.

The joy was interrupted by the delivery of a letter from Celeste.

"Dearest Father and Mother,

I must confess that I have experienced a loneliness that is at times unbearable. I miss you desperately. Things are not turning out the way I thought they would. Jobs are given to the top models. I am offered the leftovers. Criticism comes easily from people. I often think they have no concern for one's feelings. I don't think I've received a compliment since I've been here.

I am discovering that men in powerful positions expect more from a model than her flair on the runway. Other girls have told me that my survival in this business will depend largely on my willingness to go out with wealthy men who enjoy having a beautiful model on their arms for special occasions.

They expect you to loosen up with alcohol and drugs. I am resisting this. It is very uncomfortable for me. I am being

passed over when the jobs are assigned. I
must stay here. My heart longs to fulfill my
dream of being a super model.

My thoughts return to the love and
security of my family. I look forward to
spending the holidays with you.

My deepest love to all of you."
Celeste

As Philippe read the letter aloud tears ran down
Arianne's cheeks. They held each other and shared the
pain of knowing that their precious daughter was in such
emotional despair. This was what they had feared would
happen but Celeste was stubbornly determined to have her
way. All they could do now was to assure her that she could
come back home at any time. They immediately called and
gave her the love and encouragement that she needed.

Hearts were heavy in the Deriveaux home that night.
The next day Armond woke up excited about his newfound
faith.

"Little Henry told me that Jesus wants me to tell others
about my love for Him. He says that I can do that by being
baptized. Is it alright with you if I ask the preacher at the
Baptist church to baptize me soon?"

Arianne spoke up and said, "My dear son, of course that
would be fine. In fact I have been concerned that I have
not been baptized myself. It has been such a long time. I
have enjoyed worshipping with the Chandlers at the First
Baptist Church. They told me the same thing that Little
Henry told you about the importance of following Jesus in

baptism. I just have never felt like I could get up the nerve to walk down the aisle in front of everyone. But now it will be easy. I will walk down the aisle and be baptized with my handsome son. It will be an honor for me."

Plans were made for the family to attend the service on Sunday and get this settled. Arianne phoned Charlotte and told her the news.

Sunday arrived and all the Deriveauxs, including Charles, prepared for this special occasion. How they wished that Edmond and Celeste could have been with them. They sat with the Chandlers during the service. The Pastor's sermon was about Nicodemus' personal encounter with Jesus Christ. Nicodemus was a religious man. But Jesus told him that it was essential that he understand that religion and man's goodness does not make one right with God. He said, "Nicodemus, you must be born again."

Arianne noticed that her husband was uncomfortable even to the point of sweating. She reached over and took his hand and held it tightly.

After the service the Pastor greeted each person at the door of the church. Arianne introduced her son, Charles, to him. She told him how God had given him a special gift to compensate for his mental disorder.

The Pastor was amazed to hear that he played the piano, not from music in print, but from the depth of his soul. He asked if Charles would play something for him before they left. They went back into the church. Charles sat at the grand piano and heavenly music filled the sanctuary. Members of the congregation who were still on the premises made their way back in and joined the family. After Charles had finished the Pastor went to him, laid his hands on him, and blessed him in the name of the Lord. Tears of joy flowed from every eye that day. The Pastor suggested that it would be good for them to let Charles listen to great music like the Messiah as well as the beautiful classical works. He said that he would love to have Charles play some of the great hymns of the faith in their worship services. There was hesitancy on the part of Philippe because he did not know how comfortable Charles would be with a large congregation. Arianne smiled and assured her husband that God would work out all the details.

The Deriveauxs invited the Chandlers to lunch. After they ate Philippe asked Ephraim if he would join him on the veranda. His heart hungered to know more about this *Born Again experience*. Ephraim talked to him at length. Then he suggested that they set aside a time when they could open the Bible and let the answers to Philippe's question come directly from God. And they did just that. Tuesday evenings were set aside for the purpose of seeing God draw Phillipe personally to Himself.

Chapter 19

The holidays were fast approaching. It was a more prosperous time for most families. The programs attributed to F.D.R. had succeeded in putting most of the unemployed back to work. Merchants were hopeful that their stores would make up for the past lean years.

The streets were decorated with lights and garlands. Santa Claus visited Somerville early in December. The city square had a live Nativity Scene. Crowds gathered to see Mary, Joseph and the baby Jesus. The shepherds had their sheep and the Wise Men had their camels and gifts for the Christ child. Local choral groups were singing Christmas Carols. The atmosphere was alive with a spirit of love.

The Deriveauxs were anxiously anticipating the arrival of Edmond from Ole Miss. It was hard to believe that he was just a semester away from getting his law degree. They did not doubt that their bright son would pass the Bar. They called Edmond to see if he had plans to bring Leigh Ann with him. He told them that things had cooled down between the two of them. When asked why he told them that Leigh Ann found out that he was involved with someone else on the side. Leigh Ann was devastated and decided to go back to Natchez for a semester to get her emotions under control. She then planned to return to finish her education. Edmond would be gone and she could concentrate on her studies. Edmond said that as much as he cared for her he did not think that she would be his choice for a wife. He saw no point in continuing to see her exclusively.

Philippe and Arianne worried about their son. His track record was bad when it came to a monogamous relationship. They agreed that it would be best if they did not interfere in his personal affairs. After all he was twenty-five years old.

Edmond arrived the week before Christmas. Two days later Celeste flew in to the Memphis airport. The family was waiting for her with flowers and hugs. The drive back to Somerville was filled with everyone telling his or her stories. Eliza was waiting for them with a table laden with food. The appetites were satisfied in a hurry. The evening was shared with more stories and music from Charles.

The hour was late and everyone agreed that they needed a good night's sleep. How grateful they were that they would all be together for this beautiful holiday.

The one thing Arianne insisted upon was that the family attend the Christmas program at the church. The choir was performing Handel's Messiah. They wanted Charles to hear this magnificent masterpiece. Edmond and Celeste resisted but finally gave in when they realized how important it was to their mother.

Of course the Chandlers and the Middletons were there. Edmond's eyes were fixed on Daisy Chandler who was home from Smith College in the northeast. She was a sophisticated beauty just like her mother. She was not in the least impressed with this ego driven Frenchman. In his debonair style he asked Daisy if he could take her out one night. In her polite manner she told him that she would have to see what her family's plans would allow. Edmond was not used to being put off. He really wanted to get to know her better. Of course before he left the church he had also spotted Priscilla Middleton. She had just finished her first semester at the University of Tennessee. He went over to introduce himself to her. She told him about her good fortune to be given a full athletic scholarship. While talking Philippe learned of her passion for running. He asked if he might run with her one morning while they were home for the holidays. She said that she would be delighted to have him join her. She warned him that she was likened to a gazelle and would expect him to keep up with her.

The next morning Edmond called to ask when he should arrive at her house. She told him that she would be running down Levee Road and would pass his plantation. He could join her there. Edmond thought that she would not run more than a mile or two at the most. Miles later he was holding his sides and gasping for air. She was not even winded. It was Edmond's worse nightmare to appear to be inferior to a woman. Priscilla enjoyed every minute of his over inflated ego getting deflated. She took pity on him and let him stop for a rest. Laughingly she asked if he would like to call home for someone to pick him up. He was insulted at such a suggestion but asked if they could walk back home. When they arrived at the Deriveaux plantation Edmond limped into his house relieved that he did not faint from exhaustion. Priscilla stretched her hamstrings and took flight again as though she had just started. She did not have any expectations of hearing from Edmond Deriveaux again.

That was quite all right with her. His French accent fell on deaf ears. Priscilla had no time for such arrogance. Her focus was completely on continuing to train her body for competition. She very well intended to stand on the podium at the Olympics one day and have that gold medal hung around her neck. Nothing or no one would be permitted to get in the way of her goal.

Edmond collapsed when he got in the house. His mother asked him if he was okay.

"I just don't want to talk about it, thank you," he answered.

Arianne inquired, "Can I get you a glass of tea or water?"

Edmond whispered, "Yes, please. I just want to rest for awhile."

There was something that had gone awry in the Deriveaux house. Edmond was not strutting around like a rooster. Celeste was unusually reserved. Arianne had a sense that Edmond would return to his old self the next time a pretty girl responded to his advances. Celeste was another story. She felt that she had to have a mother/daughter talk. Now was as good a time as ever. After she gave Edmond his glass of iced tea she went upstairs to Celeste's room.

She knocked on the door and went in to find Celeste sitting in the window seat staring out at the river.

"Darling, do you have time to fill your mother in on your activities in New York?" she asked.

"Oh, Mommy, I feel like my life has disintegrated into shambles. My dreams of the fashion world falling at my feet have evaporated. Before I left to come home for the holidays I did something I had promised myself I would not do. I accepted a date with a rich and powerful man. We went to a new club called The Cuban Connection. I had never seen so many celebrities and politicians in my life.

It was breathtakingly elegant. The entertainment was spectacular with beautiful showgirls and some of the most famous singers and comedians. The room was smoke filled and champagne flowed freely. I danced and drank champagne until I was dizzy. The evening ended with a frightening revelation. I was told that my date was one of the top figures in the New York mafia.

Oh, Mommy, why did my agent allow this to happen? When I talked to him he just said that I needed to grow up. I was in the big city life now. The die was cast. If Tony Rizzo liked me enough to ask me out again I had better not turn him down. He doesn't take being rejected lightly.

Just before I left to come home I was told that he was trying to get in touch with me. My bags were packed and I rushed to the airport. I am terrified about going back. The models I know who have been in the business for a few years are so messed up. They will not eat much of anything but lettuce for fear they will find a fat cell on their bodies. To compensate for that they smoke and do other drugs. It seems that most of them carry a flask of vodka in their bags. Since I've been there one girl overdosed and another died from malnutrition.

Mommy, I am driven from within my soul to be a famous runway model. How can I give up my dreams? What should I do? How can I survive in such a jungle?"

Arianne held her sobbing child in her arms for a while. "Oh, my sweet little girl, how I want to take the fear and the pain from you. I know what it is to love the glamorous lifestyle of the rich and famous. But my sweet Celeste it is because we have known so little about the possibility of our need for something more. We both know what it is to be searching for perfection. But for each of us the search leads to despair instead. You got to New York and instead of fame and fortune you found fear and famine. I came to Somerville with your father seeking peace and prosperity. Before long I retreated within myself to the point of choosing to take my own life. My mind was too confused to realize that I would be leaving the family I loved with all my heart.

I hesitate to think of what would have happened if Charlotte and Eliza had not found me at just the right time. They reached out to me with loving kindness. Somehow Charlotte was able to get through to me. She told me that God loved and valued me and had a wonderful plan for my life. It was God's intervention. Otherwise I would be dead today. My darling child I must tell you the same thing. It seems that everything around you has failed you. You do not know where to turn. God wants to say to you, 'Celeste, turn to Me.' But Sweetheart you must see that for yourself."

Celeste listened intently. Tears falling down her cheeks she said, "I know you are probably right, Mother. But I just cannot see that religion would be the right thing for me. I know that I would be miserable if I had to resign myself to a life without modeling. There has to be a way for me to have my career and not succumb to the hellish environment that is pervasive in New York."

Arienne knew that she could not push her daughter any further except to explain to her the difference between religion and a personal relationship with Jesus Christ. They had been exposed to "religion" in France and Austria. In

Somerville they had seen with their eyes many people whose lives had been transformed by the power of God.

Arienne told Celeste that it was almost time for dinner. They needed to freshen up. Eliza had prepared some of the children's favorite things. Celeste thanked her mother for listening to her and for loving her unconditionally.

Chapter 20

Three years had passed since Coach Billy discovered his exceptional athlete, Priscilla Middleton. She had surpassed his wildest dreams in her development as an athlete. Now a junior at the University of Tennessee she was ready to go to the Olympic trials in Los Angeles. Coach Billy knew that she could win a place on the U.S. team in the 400 meter race. He also believed that she could qualify for a relay race. He encouraged her to go for both events. He looked forward to bringing home two gold medals. Priscilla was excited about the challenge.

When the athletes gathered for the competition all the people in Somerville stayed close to their radios. Some gathered at the barbershop; some at the beauty shop and others at the Inez Hotel coffee shop. Men gathered on the benches in front of the court house. Everyone rooted for their home town girl to qualify for the Olympics. Somerville had never had an Olympic contestant much less a gold medal winner.

Finally the eight athletes competing in the 400 meter took their places on the track. They all worked feverishly stretching their hamstrings and twisting to loosen the muscles in their bodies. Some of them bowed their heads as if they were asking for divine strength. Others appeared to be overly anxious.

The radio announcer called each runner's name and their lane. The home town people clapped and yelled when he said, "Priscilla Middleton is in lane 5. Take your marks." Priscilla stepped into her blocks and planted her feet. She put one knee on the ground to wait for the get set call. Her fingers were placed just to the edge of the starting line.

"*Get Set*", he said loudly. With an adrenalin rush she raised her knee off the ground. Her heart felt like it was going to jump out of her body. Then the sound of the gun was heard. Priscilla got off to a great start. The race was on. Her stride was perfection. The jaws were loose indicating that she was relaxed. The radio announcer was ecstatic from the beginning of the race.

"Priscilla is leaving the other runners in her dust. With every step she appeared to get stronger. If she keeps up this pace she is going to set a world record. What a spectacular sight to watch. She is perfection. And she is Olympic bound. There will be no one in the world that can come near her if she runs like this in Germany. We have witnessed the greatest runner in our lifetime."

Having easily won and established her place on the U.S. Olympic team Priscilla then set her thoughts on the 800-meter relay. Coach Billy urged those in charge to let Priscilla run the final leg. Everyone was in agreement.

Once again they took their places. The first runner did not get off to a good start for the team. When she passed the baton to the second runner a little of the lost time was made up. The third runner almost dropped the baton when it was passed to her. It was obvious that this slowed her down a few seconds. Seconds were crucial to winning the race. She passed the baton to Priscilla who at that moment was behind five of the eight runners.

Everyone watching at the trials and everyone listening to the radio broadcast felt their hearts racing. There seemed to be no chance that anyone could overcome the problem facing Priscilla. Then as if an angel picked her up from the ground she flew past one after the other. She saw the finish line with the tape across it. Her feet accelerated. There was one more runner in front of her who was fast approaching the finish line. Priscilla eased up beside her and leaned forward to break the tape and win the race.

The crowd went crazy. The radio announcer was screaming. *"Priscilla Middleton, a new name in the world of track and field, from Somerville, Mississippi, brought it home easily. I don't know how she did it. We witnessed an amazing miracle today. This young woman will go down in the record books as the most outstanding runner in the history of American sports. A new U.S. record was set that day."*

You could have heard the Somerville residents all the way to Memphis. It wasn't long before plans were in the making for a homecoming celebration for their star. The Middleton's phone was ringing off the wall. God just continued to bless this family. They had endured so much heartache for all those years. Now they were enjoying richly deserved blessings.

After the UT team returned to Knoxville they began to plan their strategy for training and winning the gold in Munich. It would be reality for them in just a few months.

Coach Billy told the team that they could go home for a week-end and then report back ready to go to work.

Priscilla got a ride to Memphis with a friend. Hoss picked her up and brought her home. Congratulations and flowers were showered on her. She was a star. Even during her three days at home she did not neglect her running. People lined up and down Levee Road to watch their local heroine run like an exquisite gazelle. She ran to the applause of her friends and family.

Chapter 21

Philippe and Arianne were awakened from a peaceful sleep by a piercing ring. Philippe felt on his nightstand for the telephone.

"The Deriveaux residence," he mumbled.

"Mr. Deriveaux, do you have a daughter named Celeste?"

"I do. And to whom am I talking to?"

"I am Dr. Cliff Watterson at Broadmore Medical Center in Manhattan. I'm afraid I have bad news for you. Your daughter was brought in to our emergency room this evening. She was unconscious. My tests showed an overdose of drugs and alcohol in her system. That combined with malnutrition caused her heart to race out of control. We have her in Cardiac Intensive Care. She does not show any positive signs of coming around. She seems to have no will to fight for her life."

Philippe interrupted, "Is my daughter going to die? Please tell me that you are going to save her life!"

"Mr. Deriveaux, we are doing everything for her medically. But she is alone. What she needs is to have someone with her who loves her and can get through to her and help her fight to live. Can you come as soon as possible?

Time is of the essence. I don't know how long her body can handle this stress."

"Dr. Watterson, I will call a friend and ask him to fly my wife and me to New York in his plane. Please don't let our child die. Tell her not to worry. Her mother and father will be there to see her through this."

He hung up the phone and with no thought of the time he called his friend, Coy Sanders. "Coy, I have just received an urgent call from a doctor in New York. Our Celeste is in critical condition in Broadmore Medical Center's CIC unit. He says that we must get there immediately. He doesn't know whether we will make it in time to speak to her. Can you fly us there?"

Coy was a fine Christian man whom Philippe had gotten to know through the Chandlers. He did not hesitate to say that he could be ready within the hour. Coy told Phillipe that he had just checked his plane out and filled it with gas the day before. He was absolutely sure that God had prompted him to get the plane in flight readiness.

Arianne had been getting dressed and packing their luggage. As soon as Philippe hung up she called Henry and Eliza. She explained what had happened and asked if one of them could come and stay with the children. Of course they would.

She then woke Vivian up. They did not think it was necessary to disturb Armond and Charles.

Henry and Eliza were at the Deriveaux's within twenty minutes. Henry drove them to the local airport where Coy was waiting for them.

Henry watched the propellers turn and the plane lift off the ground. He stayed long enough to ask God to send angels to carry them safely through the darkness. "And please, God, if it's your will let Miss Celeste come through this awful trial", he tearfully prayed.

As soon as the dawn broke Eliza called the Chandlers. Charlotte said she would get the church to call for a prayer meeting. There hearts were doubly burdened knowing that Celeste had made it clear that she had no desire to know God. Perhaps this crisis would break her stubborn will and show her how desperately she needs to know a higher power who can help her overcome her addiction. She must see that this power is God in Christ Jesus. Many Christians gathered to pray to that end.

The flight to New York seemed endless. Finally they could see the city. Coy had filed an emergency flight plan before he left Somerville giving them an estimated time of arrival. He had also requested a police escort for the Deriveauxs from the airport to the hospital. It was obvious that God had worked out all the details. A cab was waiting for them with the Escort. In record time they arrived at the hospital. Someone was waiting in the lobby to take them up the doctor's elevator to CIC. Dr. Watterson introduced himself and took them in to Celeste. Their hearts broke when they saw how thin and ashen she appeared. Tubes and I.V.s and a monitor confirmed her critical condition. They went to her bed and one on each side held her hands and kissed her forehead.

Arianne spoke first. "Celeste, my darling Celeste, it's Mother and I'm here for you. Please open your eyes and let me know that you hear me."

Philippe leaned over and put his face against his daughter's and pleaded, "You are my treasured child.

Won't you reach down and pull forth that strong will you have exercised so freely all of your life? Dear Celeste, your doctor says that your survival is dependent on your desire to live. They are doing the best they can with their medical expertise. None of that can help when your spirit chooses to give up. Fight, Celeste. Fight for your family's sake if not for your own. We need you."

Tears were streaming down both their faces. But Celeste remained motionless. Her parents were desperate to find the key to her soul.

Arianne tried once again, "Celeste, I have heard that a person can hear even when they can't acknowledge it. If you can hear me and understand what I'm saying please let me know by squeezing my hand. Darling, you are very ill. It is extremely important for me to help you understand that right now nothing matters but Jesus. He wants desperately to give you His life even when you are in such a grave situation. He doesn't require words when you are unable to speak. However, He must know that you have reached out from your spirit to receive Him into your heart. If you hear me and understand will you squeeze my hand?" Seconds passed and Celeste's weak hand seemed to squeeze her mother's.

"Now, Baby, will you choose Jesus to be your Savior?" There was no second squeeze. Arienne left the bedside broken hearted. She sat in the chair emotionally and physically exhausted and prayed.

Philippe continued to hold his child's hand hoping that somehow strength could be imparted from his body into her weak frame. About an hour had passed when once again Philippe felt Celeste's hand move. Her eyes began to struggle to open. He called for Arianne to come quickly. She ran to the bed. They saw Celeste' beautiful green eyes.

Arianne cried, "Oh, my precious baby, you are back with us. I have prayed that we might hear you speak and know that you are going to be all right. I pleaded with you to give your life to God. Did you, Celeste?"

Unable to speak above a whisper her parents leaned down to hear her long awaited words. "Runway in Paris. I'm beautiful. I love you. I'm sorry."

Celeste went back into her deep sleep. Philippe did not understand the meaning of her last words but Arienne understood all too well. They were holding each other, sobbing hysterically when they heard a loud sound from the heart monitor. They looked and saw the flat line. Doctors and nurses rushed in and called for the crash cart. They did everything they could to get her heart started again. It was too late. Celeste was gone.

Philippe and Arianne refused to leave her lifeless body until they came to take it to the morgue. Plans had to be made as to how they would get her back to Somerville. At that moment their friend Coy came to them. Not knowing what they had just gone through Coy told them about how the weather had prevented him from flying back home. He thought maybe there would be something he could do for them while he waited for permission to fly out. Philippe took his hand and thanked him for being there. He told him that Celeste had died. They were trying to decide how to get back to Somerville. Coy said he would wait for them as long as it took for them to get the body released and arrange for it to be transported on the next train. In the meantime he would fly them back home. They needed to get back as soon as possible to be with their other children. They would wait together for the body. Coy was an angel God provided to comfort this grieving couple. "We will never be able to express our gratitude for your kindness," sobbed Arianne.

The next thing that had to be done was to call home. Eliza answered the phone.

"Eliza, this is Phillipe. We have sad news. Our Celeste has passed on."

Eliza screamed, "Oh, no, Mr. Phillipe. Don't you go saying something like that! Miss Celeste ain't no more than twenty years old. She ain't lived long enough to be ready to die. Please tell me you done made a mistake in what you said."

"It's no mistake, Eliza. Don't tell the children until we get there. We must do that. Coy is going to fly us back home. We will need to take care of the hospital business. We are not going to Celeste' apartment now. We will make a trip back later to take care of such details. We just want to get home to our family and friends. We need your love and support."

"Now, Mr. Phillipe, you knows you got that. We gonna be praying for your safety. God's gonna send his angels to bring you back safely," said Eliza.

Phillipe asked Coy to take Arianne to the coffee shop and try to get her to eat something. "She must take care of herself now. I will go and talk to the doctors and get releases and attend to the business details. Then I will join you."

In less than four hours Coy was in flight carrying his friends back home. It broke his heart to see their pain. He had children of his own and could imagine that there would be nothing harder than to say good-bye to one of them. He did not know that the greatest pain was not that Celeste had died. It was that she had continued to refuse God's invitation to come to Him. With her dying words she chose the world and its fleeting fame over a personal relationship with Jesus Christ. This was so final. They had no hope of seeing her again in heaven.

The mind cannot fathom the seemingly endless number of hours it took for them to fly home. Coy suggested that they try to sleep while they had the chance. When they arrived at their home there would be so many questions that needed answers. The telephone would be ringing. Rest would be almost impossible for these two exhausted parents.

They finally landed on the small airstrip in Somerville. Coy had left his car there. He drove them home. Words had been minimal. Shock would have described the demeanor of the Deriveauxs.

As they drove up the winding tree lined drive to the mansion they could see Henry and Eliza come out the front door. They had been watching for over an hour. Philippe and Arianne got out of Coy's car and embraced their faithful friends. Everyone knew that these weary people needed to just go inside and hold their children before they shared their sad news.

Vivian and Armond ran to their parents. Philippe held them tightly as if to protect them from any more pain than was necessary.

"Children you know we went to New York to be with your sister. She was very ill. The doctors did everything possible to help restore her to good health. They were not successful. Our Celeste lost her battle for life."

Both the children burst out crying. "No, Papa, Celeste is too young to die. She said that she was going to be a famous fashion model. Papa, you have made a mistake," cried Vivian.

Armond stood up straight and wiped his tears and said, "Papa, I will get Little Henry to ask God to let her live. He knows how to pray and God answers his prayers. I'll call him right now."

"Armond, my son, even Little Henry's prayers cannot bring our Celeste back. We will have to pray that God will give us the grace to accept this sorrow. Together we are going to get through this. I promise you that."

Eliza brought coffee and freshly baked blueberry muffins for the family. As they sat down to refresh themselves they heard a sweet melody coming from the music room. Arianne went in and put her arms around Charles as he continued to play. He was playing, *Savior, like a Shepherd lead us.* She recalled that this was sung the last time they attended church. The pastor was right when he suggested that they expose Charles to hymns of the faith so that he would include them in his gifted repertoire. She remembered some of the lyrics...*Much we need Thy tender care. In Thy pleasant pastures feed us. For our use Thy folds prepare.*

She rushed back into the parlor and shared with the family that God had given them a word of encouragement through their special child. For a little while heavy hearts were lightened.

The next call that needed to be made was to Ephraim and Charlotte. They would know how to make plans for a memorial service for Celeste when her body arrived. Phillipe and Arianne wanted a small gathering of family and close friends. Their desire was to have family members eulogize their daughter. They would like for the pastor to pray for their family. They did not want it to be lengthy. There was nothing left for them to do except to say their final good-byes.

One week later they gathered at the church. Edmond had come home to be with his family. The Chandlers, the Joneses, the Middletons and a large number of other friends were there. Philippe's cousin, Jean Paul and his family came from New Orleans. The pastor said a few words on behalf of the family and asked Charles to play the piano before the eulogies. To their surprise he played *The Old Rugged Cross.* This was another song he had heard sung in church.

Philippe got up first to speak. "Never did I think I would stand before you in church with a broken heart over the absence of one of my children. Parents think they will pass on first and their children will bury them. This is out of order. I do not understand why my daughter's young life was taken. I do know that there will be a permanent hole in my heart that will never heal. My children were born in France. I brought them to Somerville to give them the opportunity to grow up in a country filled with opportunities. I thought it would be utopia. It was not long after we settled in Somerville that the news came as a result of the market crash this country plummeted into a deep depression. Our family fared very well and I still felt we were on top of the world. My children grew up and my son Edmond has his law degree and is on his own in a prominent law firm. Celeste was our second child and knew from the time she was a young girl that she was destined to be a famous fashion model.

Her mother and I tried to convince her that she needed to get a college education first. We finally realized that she was going to pursue her dream even if she had to leave home to do it. She had no idea that anymore would be asked of her except to stay thin and beautiful and be ready to travel at any given moment. She saw herself in Paris and Milan modeling for the most famous designers.

As she was dying, her last words to us were: "Runway in Paris. I love you. I'm sorry." Her dream turned out to be a vapor. I will forever ask myself what more I could have done to dissuade her from the thing that would destroy her. Forgive me my dear Celeste. You were my treasure, my beautiful flower, my daughter."

Edmond spoke next. "I have always had great admiration for my sister. She was one who knew the path her life was to take. She was not intimidated as she walked up that path. I don't understand what death is all about. I don't know whether there is life after death. But I do know that Celeste filled her twenty-one years with exactly what she desired. I regret that she died before she saw her dream become reality. I will miss her."

It was Vivian's turn to share her thoughts. "Celeste was a unique older sister. It was like living with a larger than life presence. The way she carried herself as she walked was like ballet in motion. A hair was never out of place and her makeup was impeccable. I have to admit that I was often a bit jealous of her sense of self-confidence. She always encouraged me to dream my dreams and then go after them with everything in me.

We didn't have the same dreams. Mine have been quite different. As I remember her today I am thankful for the things I learned from her. Don't let anything get you down. Don't let anyone keep you from your destiny. Know your heart and be true to it. I will miss my sister greatly. Her place in my heart will never fade."

Arianne and Armond knew that their thoughts had already been expressed. They chose to keep their thoughts for a later time.

Everyone left the church and made their way to the cemetery where Celeste's body was laid to rest. They would decide on an appropriate tombstone at a later date.

Family and friends went back to the Deriveaux's where some of the sadness was dispelled as they sat and shared good memories of their loved one.

Chapter 22

Day after day, Millicent's concern for Ellen grew stronger. It seemed that her anti-social behavior drove her into a reclusive state. When she joined the family for a meal she sat quietly and picked at her food. Millicent tried to think of the special meals she could prepare to please her child. Occasionally she would seem to enjoy a fried chicken pulley bone or believe it or not she liked fried chicken livers. She was bone thin and prone to succumb to every cold virus that came through Somerville.

After each meal, the three girls were responsible for cleaning the kitchen. You could hear them say: "I bids to put away. I bids to dry." The last one had to wash the dishes. Melanie seemed to win the easiest job of putting them away. Priscilla usually got the drying. Because Ellen's mind was always in her reading or writing she ended up having to wash the dishes. As soon as she finished her chore she excused herself and returned to her room.

Two years had passes since Edmond graduated from Law School and passed the Bar Exam. His grades, his social status, and his debonair personality assured him of a job in a prominent law firm in Jackson.

Philippe and Arienne felt confident that he would find stability in this new environment. Their hope was that he would meet the right person for him, fall in love, and then marry. For years they had been troubled by his philandering.

After several months at the firm of Jones, Langdon and Myers, he was assigned to go to a conference on *Ethics in Politics* at the Edwards Hotel. Edmond had always had a deep passion for politics so this was a great assignment. After the first session, they adjourned for lunch in the formal dining room.

He noticed another large group nearby. As was his custom he gave the *once over* to all the women. Much to his surprise and delight right there in the midst of the group was Leigh Ann. It had been a long time since the days at Ole Miss. He had never forgotten her.

Leigh Ann looked toward his table and their eyes met and locked. Each one got up from their table. They met half way with their arms outstretched. As they hugged one another the distance that had been between them disappeared. Lunch was the last thing on their minds.

"What are you doing here?" Edmond asked Leigh Ann.

"I am working for a public relations firm in Natchez. We are meeting with several large corporations to try and convince them that Mississippi would be a perfect location for them. Natchez could offer them the benefits of the Mississippi River. What are you doing in Jackson, Edmond?"

"I passed the bar and was fortunate enough to start my career with a prestigious firm here in Jackson. This conference I'm attending is exciting since I hope to go into politics one day."

They continued to talk for a while and noticed that their groups were leaving the dining hall. They didn't mind that they had missed lunch. Both of them had to get back to their next session. Before they parted they agreed to meet that evening for dinner. There was much they needed to catch up on in a short time. They agreed on Primo's on Capitol Street at 6:00 P.M.

The anticipation was overwhelming for both of them. The hour finally arrived. They were sitting at the table of Edmond's choice. It was dimly lit and out of the main traffic pattern. Edmond arrived first. When Leigh Ann arrived he met her with a kiss.

Edmond's French roots did not hesitate to bring a bottle of fine French wine. Even though alcoholic beverages were not sold in the restaurant he persuaded, with a generous tip, the headwaiter to bring them two wine glasses. Leigh Ann had never had a drink of any kind but she felt that this was a special occasion. As they shared memories of their days at Ole Miss they found that they were completely at ease with each other. The physical attraction was definitely still alive. After dinner and finishing the bottle of wine Edmond insisted on driving Leigh Ann back to the Edwards Hotel. He asked if he might come up to her room so that they could just talk a bit longer. She agreed.

When they got to her room it seemed so natural to embrace and to feel their lips together once again. The wine had broken down Leigh Ann's strength to say no to this young man she had loved all these years. The flesh took control and the passion was released. Edmond was shocked to discover that Leigh Ann was not a virgin. Through a flood of tears she explained to him how devastated she was when he had cheated on her. When she left Ole Miss and went home to Natchez she felt betrayed. She began to wonder about what she had gained from being such a *good girl.* Her old boyfriend was hoping she would come back to him. She sought comfort in his arms and in a moment of passion she relinquished the most precious thing she possessed to one who knew would never be her husband. Her desire was always to give her virginity as a wedding gift to her husband. The guilt of that mistake had plagued her since it happened.

Leigh Ann asked Edmond to tell her the truth. "Does this mean that you still love me and that we have a future together?"

It hurt Edmond to be truthful but he knew that he had to. He answered, "Leigh Ann, I have always had deep feelings and real passion for you. I admired the stand you took in college when you refused to let me have my way with you. But if I am to be totally honest my focus is on my career. There is much I plan to do before I seriously consider marriage. I am sure that if my hunger to be in politics becomes a reality it will be imperative for me to choose a suitable wife for a Washington society politician. That person must be from the right family with power and sophistication. I know that that is not the best formula for a loving family environment. You would be my choice if that were the case. But I can't turn back from my dreams of possibly being in the Senate of the United States. I would resent you if I were restrained in any way from succeeding in this endeavor."

Leigh Ann was devastated. "Why did you lead me on in this way if that is the way you feel? You think I am not acceptable? You are the lowest form of humanity! You are a self-centered, egotistical jackass! I never want to lay eyes on you again."

She was screaming and crying at the same time. He reached out to comfort her. She drew back and with all her strength she slapped his face and beat on his chest. "Get out of my room!" she screamed. "I hope you rot in hell!"

Edmond left and returned to his apartment. It was a sleepless night for both of them. He was at a loss to understand Leigh Ann's reaction. What did she expect from him? One night of pleasure should lead to marriage? Her emotional outburst made no sense to him.

Leigh Ann cried through the night. She could not understand how someone she loved so deeply could have ice water running through his veins. How could anyone be content to have an arranged marriage for the sake of promoting himself in the political world? What a mistake she had made in thinking that he really cared about her.

For two months she sweated the fact that they had not used contraception. What was the possibility that she might be pregnant? She was tormented by all the possibilities of the consequences of their indiscretion.

Her worse fears came to light when she missed her period. Not wanting to think of what this meant she put off going to her doctor. Another month passed before she accepted the fact that she had to do something right away. Edmond had made it painfully clear that he was not interested in marrying her. Her faith would not permit her to consider an abortion that was probably what he would insist on if he found out she was pregnant.

Leigh Ann cried herself to sleep several nights in a row. One morning she woke up fighting mad. This was not just her problem. She knew that if Edmond did not have the integrity to own up to his responsibility she would have to go to his parents. She called the Deriveauxs and asked if they could meet her in Jackson. The matter was too sensitive to discuss over the phone. Sensing the urgency in her voice Philippe said they could be in Jackson by noon the following day.

Leigh Ann told her parents that a business meeting had come up. She would have to go to Jackson. Since this was not unusual for their daughter they thought nothing of it.

The meeting took place in the dining room at the Edwards Hotel, where Leigh Ann had fallen for Edmond's charm just two months before.

Leigh Ann arrived first and nervously awaited the Deriveauxs.

"Mr. and Mrs. Deriveaux, thank you for coming. I am sorry to be mysterious. I needed to talk to you face to face."

Arianne said softly, "My dear child, of course we would come. You sounded extremely anxious. Whatever is the problem?"

Leigh Ann poured out her heart to them not leaving out essential details. They were all too familiar with their son's out of control libido. Fortunately they had not had to deal with a pregnancy.

Arianne put her arms around Leigh Ann to comfort her. "You dear girl, how can we ever tell you how sorry we are that our son has brought this trial upon you. We are aware of his selfishness and have grieved over our inability to get through to him about the consequences of his impulsive behavior. He never learns. He continues to live as though he has a right to take whatever he feels will satisfy his immediate need. He doesn't seem to care about who he hurts in the process. This baby you are carrying is innocent. We totally agree with you that this child has every right to live. And abortion is not an option."

They told her to go home and give them a few days to think it through. They promised to get back to her very soon.

Philippe and Arianne talked non-stop from Jackson to Somerville. They sought the wise counsel of their friends, Ephraim and Charlotte. After seeking God's direction through prayer they were at peace about the best way to deal with the matter. This baby had Deriveaux blood running through those little veins. He or she would be raised a Deriveaux.

First plans were made for Leigh Ann to leave Natchez before anyone suspected that she was pregnant. A call was placed to Jean Paul, Philippe's cousin in New Orleans. He was filled in on the whole situation. His business was located in New Orleans with offices in Paris, France. He called Leigh Ann and offered her a lucrative job as a public relations representative handling business between New Orleans and Paris. This was perfectly suited to her expertise. It would not be unusual for her not to be able to make a trip back to Mississippi for at least a year. The baby would be born in Paris.

This problem solved there would be time now for details to be worked out so that Philippe and Arianne would be told about a little baby who was put up for adoption. They would anxiously proceed with plans for the adoption. Arianne had longed to have another little baby to cherish. Philippe would rest in the knowledge that his grandson would be raised in the manner appropriate for a Deriveaux. Leigh Ann would have the choice of remaining in Paris or returning to New Orleans with a guaranteed job with Deriveaux Imports. There would surely be times when she could see the child. But she would sign away any right to ever acknowledge that she was the birth mother.

The plan was put into operation. Within two weeks, Leigh Ann was on her way to Paris. She knew in her heart that she was doing the best thing for everyone especially her little baby. That truth did not erase the pain she felt deep in her soul. She cried many tears knowing that she would not be the one who would nurse this precious child. She would never tuck him in at night and sing a lullaby to him. As he learned to walk she would not be there to pick him up when he fell. She could not take him to school that first day or see him graduate twelve years later. Her thoughts were overwhelming to the point of depression. Then she would remember that what she was doing was the best gift she could give her baby. She knew he would have a secure home with loving parents. That knowledge would be her comfort for the next seven months.

The voyage seemed endless. Most of the days were spent in her cabin. Jean Paul accompanied her. He insisted that she join him for their meals. She knew that the baby needed nourishment even though she felt like she could not swallow solid food.

The long awaited day arrived. She looked out her porthole and saw the sun rising over a panoramic view of France. Leigh Ann had never been out of Mississippi. Her heart seemed to leap up into her throat. Jean Paul knocked on her door.

"Leigh Ann, Look out your port hole and see your first view of France."

Leigh Ann rushed to the door. "I have seen it already, Jean Paul. It is exciting to know that we have finally arrived," replied Leigh Ann.

"Get your things together for the porter. He will see that they are taken to shore."

Leigh Ann said, "My luggage has been packed for some time. I have not been able to sleep."

Jean Paul informed her that breakfast would be served before they departed the ship. "I'll wait for you in the dining room," he said.

"I will be ready soon," replied Leigh Ann. She was thrilled to be leaving the self-inflicted confinement of the small cabin. She checked the cabin carefully to make sure that she didn't overlook something. Then she hurried to the dining hall. A lovely breakfast of crepes and fresh fruit were just right to settle her nervous stomach.

Before debarking the ship at the port of Le Havre, Jean Paul and Leigh Ann expressed thanks to the captain for the care that was taken by all the crew to make their voyage as comfortable as possible.

Philippe Deriveaux's parents met them at the port. Everything about them spoke loudly of their affluence. They were greeted with a kiss on each cheek. Introductions were made. Instead of driving to Paris much to Leigh

Ann's surprise they were whisked away to a huge yatch. The Deriveauxs thought that it would be a gracious way to welcome their houseguest by traveling to Paris on the Seine River. Leigh Ann found it difficult to articulate her thoughts. She not only felt dowdy in the presence of French couturier but she had never in all her life seen such luxury as she saw in this yatch. She was not allowed to carry anything heavier than her purse. Someone was serving her things to eat and drink constantly. All she could think of was how she was going to live through the next seven months without dispelling all doubt that she was illiterate in their sophisticated European ways. She was thoroughly out of her comfort zone. The dye was cast. She would have to pray that God would get her through this challenge.

The Deriveaux family exuded loving kindness to their houseguest. The best pre-natal care was provided for Leigh Ann. They took her on short trips to different places in the vicinity of their home. Of course they made sure that she saw the Eiffel Tower, the Arc de Triomphe, and Notre Dame. The museums with paintings by the master artist fascinated her. Sidewalk cafes and shopping were some of her favorite things. She even developed a love for the opera. Natchez had not been exposed to authentic opera.

The Deriveauxs took their guest down to Bordeaux near the Bay of Biscayne into the wine country. The highlight of Leigh Ann's stay was the trip to Montpellier where the Deriveauxs had a summerhouse. It was located on the Gulf of Lion. This body of water went into the Mediterranean Sea. The views were glorious and the walks along the beach were blissfully soothing.

Much to Leigh Ann's surprise, she was told to put on her beautiful new dresses she had purchased on the many shopping trips to the fashion houses in Paris. She must look ravishing for their special guests, the Duke and Duchess of Windsor, who were coming to Tea. The only thing she knew was that the Duke left England's throne to marry Wallis Simpson, an American divorcee.

Leigh Ann chose a navy A-line dress with a large white cowl collar. Her body had not reached the place where she could not compensate for pregnancy. The dress had striking gold buttons down the front. She accessorized with gold earrings and bracelets.

When she went downstairs feeling like she could hold her own with the royal guests she was shocked. There stood the Duchess in furs, diamonds and of all things, a wide brimmed hat. Once again Leigh Ann was reminded of her roots good though they were they were a long way from the sophistication of English royalty.

Tea and fancy French pastries were served in the parlor. Leigh Ann said very little but listened intently to all the conversations. She had seen and heard things on the news in Natchez about the events of the 1936 Olympics. Hitler made it known that he was the Fuehrer of the superior white race in Germany. Everyone knew how enraged he was when Jesse Owens proved his superiority in the Olympic track and field events.

Leigh Ann was shocked to hear the former King of England, Edward VIII talking about his friendship and admiration for Adolph Hitler. Apparently, Hitler had mesmerized influential leaders, including Winston Churchill, across Europe. They did not see how his crazed mind had no intention of sparing France or England. It was not until the bomb began to explode that they saw his evil heart.

Leigh Ann was impressed when she heard that the former King was the first member of British royalty to become a pilot. He had served in World War I.

Leigh Ann asked one question, "How is it that you live in France instead of England?"

Wallis, now called the Duchess, answered, "He adored me. My desire was to live here and my wish was his command. I abhorred the fact that Edward's family looked down their royal noses at me. What do we need with their abuse?"

The Duke and Duchess paid little attention to Leigh Ann. The afternoon finally came to an end. Kisses on cheeks were exchanged between the Deriveauxs and the Duke and Duchess of Windsor. Leigh Ann was bypassed.

Days quickly turned into weeks and weeks into months. Leigh Ann's body changed drastically. The once tiny size six began to look like she had swallowed a beach ball. It got increasingly more difficult to get up and down. Sometimes she felt as though the baby was pressing on her lungs making it hard to breathe. Nights were miserable and days were not much better. She was sure that her baby was a boy and was going to be a famous soccer player. His kick was torture.

One night an intense pain awakened her. Her first thought was that it might be a labor pain. Then she realized that the due date was two weeks away. She tried to go back to sleep. There was another sharp pain. This time she sat up on the side of the bed. It seemed that maybe thirty minutes elapsed between the pains. Since this was her first pregnancy, she was afraid to take a chance. A bell had been placed on her nightstand so that she could call if she needed something. She rang the bell. Minutes later there was a knock on her door.

"Leigh Ann, can I come in?" asked Mrs. Deriveaux.

"Yes, please, I need you to help me understand what is happening to me."

Mrs. Deriveaux sat on the bed and Leigh Ann told her about the pains. "We can't take any chances, Mrs. Deriveaux told her. Go to the bathroom and get ready to go to the hospital. I must tell my husband to make arrangements for the car to be brought to the door. Then I will return to help you". Before Mrs. Deriveaux left the room, Leigh Ann got up but did not make it to the bathroom before her water broke. Mrs. Deriveaux screamed for her husband. She could not leave Leigh Ann now. It was imperative that they get her on the way to the hospital immediately.

Mr. Deriveaux carried Leigh Ann down the long spiral mahogany staircase. They put a blanket over her and rushed her to St. Joan's Medical Center. There was not a minute to spare. Her obstetrician arrived shortly before the Deriveauxs. Leigh Ann was taken to the delivery room. She was fully dilated. She was told to take some deep breaths. Dr. Marquette told her to follow his instructions. He would tell her when to push. After two pushes he announced that he saw the head. One more push and a little boy came out of his mother's small womb into a big world. Dr. Marquette said, "Leigh Ann, you have a healthy son with ten fingers and ten toes. He is yelling already and a feisty little fellow he is."

He placed her baby in her arms. Tears flowed down her face. There was relief that she had given birth to this perfect child. The joy was clouded by the realization that he belonged to her for only a short time. It would not be long before she recuperated enough to make the trip back across the ocean. She knew when she arrived at New Orleans Philippe and Arianne Deriveaux, her baby's grandparents would take him home with them to Somerville. Everything would be in place for them to adopt him as their son. The baby's biological father, Edmond, would be able to see him grow up.

She was his biological mother. It devastated her that she was going to give up all her rights to be there for him through his formative years. She did not know how anyone could cry as many tears as she had cried. Deep in her heart she knew still that she was doing what was best for her son. She knew that even though he had another name and lived in another city it would never alter the truth that she was and would always be his mother.

For the few weeks that she had with him before she was physically able to travel home she had the joy of breastfeeding him. She could sing to him and hold him until she had to put him in his basinet. She determined to make a collection of memories that she could call from her heart when the pain of their separation got too heavy for her.

Many pictures were made during the first weeks of his life. Some were made in the christening gown that was worn by all the Deriveaux children through several generations. When the day came for Leigh Ann and her baby to leave France Jean Paul was there to accompany her back to the states. It was decided that Philippe and Arianne would choose the name for their adopted son. His name will be Jean Luc.

Leigh Ann gave her baby a special name. I will always think of him and call him Angel. In my heart I know God gave me my Angel. I will treasure His gift all the days of my life.

Mr. and Mrs. Deriveaux gave a beautifully wrapped gift to Leigh Ann as she left their home to go and board the ship. They told her to wait until she and Jean Luc were in their cabin before she opened it.

Departure time arrived. Jean Paul and Leigh Ann waved to the Deriveauxs as the ship pulled out of port. Leigh Ann carried Jean Luc to their cabin. After putting her baby to bed she opened her gift. It was an exquisite gold locket with a beautifully carved Madonna and Child on a heart. When she opened the locket she saw the sweetest picture of Jean Luc. Out of all the pictures they made and gave to Leigh Ann this was her favorite. There was a note inside the box. It read, *Our dear Leigh Ann, you have made the ultimate sacrifice for your precious child. We are in awe of your courage and generosity. Please be assured of our prayers for your future. Never forget that there will be a great reunion when we get to Heaven. Your baby cannot be taken from your heart. Remember this each time you open your locket. Say a prayer then for Jean Luc. He is indeed your Angel.*

The voyage from France to New Orleans seemed to fly by. Leigh Ann did not want to waste any time. In fact, she stayed awake most of the nights. Her eyes were fixed on her sleeping Angel. It was imperative that she absorb every detail so that she could at least have the memories to comfort her.

The tears were confined to the nights. Joy filled her days with him.

The inevitable arrival in the New Orleans port came too soon.

Awaiting them were Philippe, Arianne, and Jean Paul's wife, Marie. Arianne embraced Leigh Ann. One look at Angel won her heart. He looked exactly like Edmond when he was a baby. She did not immediately reach for the baby. As a mother she knew the pain it would cause Leigh Ann if someone took her baby too soon. She had to feel a freedom to release him.

After retrieving their luggage they drove to Jean Paul's estate in old New Orleans. There Leigh Ann was able to gently put her baby in Arianne's arms. Each of his relatives took their turn holding him and *oohing and aahing* over this handsome child. Compassion compelled Arienne to arrange for Angel to stay in Leigh Ann's room.

The next morning was time enough for Jean Luc (Angel) to leave with his grandparents and go to his home in Somerville. Leigh Ann kissed her Angel. She told him, "My baby, my Angel, I will never forget you. I will pray for you every day of my life. Your picture in my locket will be a visual reminder of the few weeks I was privileged to care for you. You indeed are a gift from God. I must share this gift with your new parents. They will love you and give you a blessed life. I will find a way to live with the regrets of your conception that caused me to be forced to give you up. I love you with a deeper love than I ever knew was possible."

She then placed her baby in his new mother's arms. She stayed composed until they drove down the long driveway. Then she fainted from the exhaustion of the stress and her sleep deprived state. Jean Paul picked her up and carried her back into his home. Marie got cold wet compresses to place on her head. Their doctor was called. The diagnosis was extreme mental, emotional and physical stress. He told them that she would need careful monitoring. Depression would follow the trauma of losing her baby. She could possibly begin to think of suicide.

The decision was made for Leigh Ann to spend a month or two with Jean Paul and Marie. Before she could go back to her family in Natchez she would have to be emotionally stable. They would help her to adhere to a good nutritional diet and systematic exercise in order to get back to her size 6.

Leigh Ann's depression led her into the darkest corner on the planet. The Deriveaux's cook prepared the most delectable New Orleans cuisine for their houseguest. It was delicious but too rich for Leigh Ann's deprived stomach. Authentic Jewish chicken soup finally hit the spot. To heal the stomach was not enough. Her heart had to be healed. The most prominent psychiatrist in New Orleans was called to help Leigh Ann find her way back to a sound mind. The therapy was intensive but ultimately successful. She had to be able to forgive herself for the mistake she made with Edmond at the Edward's Hotel in Jackson. The baby she conceived was of great value and would grow up to contribute something special to his world.

It was now time for Leigh Ann to go home. The Deriveaux staff packed her clothes. Jean Paul insisted on driving her to Natchez.

They arrived at her home. The door was open. She entered with some anticipation as to how she would hide the pain in her heart from them. Surely they would be aware of the sadness that she could not just wish away.

Hearing the door open her Mother left her ironing and went to the foyer. "Leigh Ann, what in the world are you doing here. We thought you were still in Paris. When did you get back to Mississippi? How long can you stay?" Questions rolled out of her mouth not giving her daughter an opportunity to answer each one.

"Mama, slow down now. Let me put my luggage down and take a deep breath and just look at you. Then I will fill you in on all the details."

"All right, Baby, but we can't wait to hear all about your job in Paris. But first, I'm gonna get you a big glass of iced tea. Would you like a piece of gingerbread cake to go with it?"

"No, thank you, Mama, I just want to rest. It's been a very long and stressful time. I really just need a soft place to fall."

"Honey, you just take all the time you need. Your Daddy and I will be right here when you feel like talking."

At five o'clock, Leigh Ann's father returned home from work. Much to his surprise and joy his little girl was asleep on the couch. Not wanting to awaken her he hurried to the kitchen to find out from his wife about what had happened.

"Darlin, I don't know what to tell you. She just showed up unexpectedly. She was exhausted. She drank some tea and ate a little gingerbread and fell fast asleep. We'll talk to her when she wakes up."

When Leigh Ann woke up she went to the kitchen. Seeing her father was overwhelming to her. She threw her arms around him and burst into tears.

"Baby, what's wrong with you. This ain't no time to be crying. We've got our little girl back home where she belongs. You've been gone way too long. We are going to take care of you and don't you forget it. We love you, baby girl."

"Oh, Daddy, I feel so safe when your strong arms around me. I have missed my home. I've missed Natchez. This is my sanctuary, my peaceful, private, and protected place. I have thanked God over and over for the parents He gave me. Now I want to make sure that you both know how much I love you."

They all sat down together. Leigh shared many of the things she had experienced while abroad. Her job was very rewarding. She had been privileged to see many awesome sights. She told them about the gracious French hospitality and the rich and powerful people she was exposed to at social gatherings. Her parents could not believe the stories they were hearing. That was a far cry from anything most people from Natchez could fathom. There was one part of her year that she could never share with her parents. They could never know the truth about their first grandchild, "Angel." They would never feel his little soft body in their arms or see his beautiful face with those big brown eyes looking back at them. No and their ears would never hear the *Coos*. This was the secret Leigh Ann must always carry in her heart. But the questions would haunt her, "Can the Deriveaux affluence fill the place in a child's heart that belongs only to his mother? And can the mother ever find something that will fill that emptiness in her heart?"

Her search for the answers to these questions began the day that she gave up her legal rights to her baby.

Joy filled the home of Philippe and Arianne Deriveaux. It had been two months since they brought little Jean Luc from New Orleans to Somerville. Many sad things had happened to this family. Arianne's depression that led her to attempt suicide was devastating. Something beautiful had come out of this tragedy when she gave her heart to Jesus Christ. Since that time she had been the strength in this family. Their handsome son, Charles, a savant, had been a constant challenge for the family. Although they were proud of his musical genius they still had sorrow because of his being mentally and emotionally challenged. They knew that he would never fall in love, marry and have children of his own. Then each time they remembered their beautiful Celeste who sacrificed her life for something as worthless as a modeling career, they wept. The greatest pain was the knowledge that she had refused God's gift of salvation and eternal security. Edmond aggressively followed his passion for politics by getting his law degree and laying the groundwork by aligning himself with a prominent law firm in Jackson. Philippe and Arianne knew that he was a self-centered womanizer who did not think twice about getting what he wanted even if it hurt someone else. He only had a conscience of convenience and no conscience of conviction. Leigh Ann was just one of many he had tossed aside and never looked back.

Then there were the two children who had given them no problems. Vivian had the good fortune to fall in love with Ephraim and Charlotte's son, Ben. The Chandlers had raised their children to know and love God from the time they were in their mother's womb. Charlotte would sing spiritual songs and read portions of scripture to each child.

These children had wonderful role models who didn't just talk about their faith they lived out their faith.

When the Deriveauxs moved to Somerville and were introduced to the Chandlers, Ben could not take his eyes off Vivian. They were the same age and in many of the same classes and activities at school. Vivian thought Ben was the most handsome young man she had ever seen. It was not long before Ben asked her to go church with him. Afterwards she had many questions to ask him. Her religious experiences had been going to mass in musty cathedrals in Paris. People in this Baptist church were so happy. Everybody seemed to sing from deep down in their hearts. The preacher was easy to understand. It was English and not Latin. Her first question was, "Is this really religion?"

Ben did not push anything on Vivian. He just simply answered her naïve questions. It did not take long for her to understand the fundamental teachings of Christianity as it is laid out in the Bible. The day came when Vivian asked Ben to tell her how she could become a believer. He always carried his New Testament with him. He opened it to Romans and led his sweetheart to Jesus. The Deriveauxs now had three believers, Arienne, Vivian and Armond.

Armond was their youngest child until Jean Luc joined the family. Armond's best friend Little Henry did not waste any time helping his buddy know about God's love for him. Vivian and Armond were baptized together with their loving families there to witness their public profession of their faith in Jesus Christ as their Lord and Savior.

Who would be next? Philippe or Edmond? They knew that God's grace was extended to Charles in a special salvation. He did not understand anything about man's sin and rejection of God. He was like a little child who never reached the age of accountability. Ephraim was spending time with Philippe sharing in bible study. Philippe did not find it easy to accept things that he could not see or understand. Ephraim explained that the Bible says that faith is the substance of things hoped for and the evidence of things unseen. Without faith it is impossible to please God. He would explain over and over that *faith was simply believing God and what God had declared in His Word, the Bible.* Ephraim assured Philippe of his prayers daily for him to let God open his spirit eyes and his spirit ears so that he could see and hear God speak to his heart. Everyone knew that it would not be long before Philippe would repent of his sins and turn to Jesus. The family needed him to be the strong spiritual head of their home. Everyone knew that salvation could not be accomplished because of the work of a godly man like Ephraim or a gentle, loving wife like Arianne, or even a spiritual giant like little Henry. If it was to be life changing it must be the work of the Holy Spirit of God. And so they waited and prayed.

Now the family had the privilege of welcoming little Jean Luc into their lives. No one except Philippe and Arianne knew the circumstances of his birth. All they knew was that Jean Paul knew of a little baby who needed a wonderful home. The story was told that he knew Arianne wanted another child but was unable to conceive. When she heard about this newborn baby she did not hesitate to say they would love to adopt him. No one who heard the story had trouble believing it. Philippe, Arianne, Jean Paul and his household, and Leigh Ann would keep their silence forever. Even Edmond would never know Jean Luc was his son.

Arianne, with Eliza's help, had created a nursery that looked like it was prepared for a prince. The gilded French bassinet with white eyelet covers stood in the center of the room. Surrounding it was a gold trimmed chest with matching armoire. Each drawer was filled with designer clothes fit for royalty. An elegant twin brass bed also covered with eyelet was added to the room for Mary, Eliza's daughter. She was given the pleasure of being Jean Luc's nanny. Of course there was an antique rocking chair for cradling this special little bundle of joy.

It was not long before friends from all over Somerville began to come knocking on their door anxious to meet the new little Deriveaux. Jean Luc seemed to enjoy the attention. He was the sweetest little angel ever sent from Heaven.

Chapter 23

Four years had passed since Coach Billy took Priscilla to the University of Tennessee. The training regimen he put his protégé through was rigid. Priscilla was no physical wimp. She had worked all her life in cotton fields. After working all day she then embarked on running through the countryside. This was not laborious to her. It was her way of releasing stress. She was alone and in control of her life. Coach Billy never heard Priscilla complain about long hours and hard work.

Each year proved him right. She was exceptionally gifted. All this work took her easily to the 1936 Olympics in Berlin, Germany. That day finally came. Coach Billy and Priscilla joined many others from the United States on a ship headed for Europe. Athletes from across the U.S. bonded on their long journey. One of the young athletes was from Alabama. His name was Jesse Owens. Coach Billy had heard about Jesse from many of his fellow coaches. Everyone agreed that Jesse was our greatest hope for gold medals.

Some of the athletes shunned Jesse because of his race. Priscilla had been raised in a racially prejudiced environment. However her second family was the Jones family. Mary and Sarah Jones were her closest friends. She could never understand why anyone would treat the Joneses as though they were inferior. On one level she could identify with this ugliness. Priscilla's own family was looked down on by many simply because they were poor and not always able to attend school. Some bad mannered children made fun of them and called them stupid. This pain made the Middleton children work harder to prove that they were as intelligent as anyone in Somerville. Priscilla felt a sense of satisfaction when she not only completed her four years of study at the University of Tennessee but graduated with honors. To top it off she was on her way to the Olympics with great anticipation of winning at least one, maybe two, Gold Medals.

By the time the athletes arrived in Munich, Coach Billy, Priscilla and Jesse were close friends. Hopes were high. Excitement was in the hearts of every participant. The International Olympic committee, IOC, had awarded the games to Berlin in 1931 with no idea that Adolf Hitler was to take power in Germany two years later. By 1936 the Nazis had control over Germany and had already begun to implement their racist policies.

Under these circumstances boycotting the Olympics was debated internationally. The United States strongly considered boycotting but accepted the invitation at the last minute.

The Nazis took advantage of the event to promote their ideology. The stadiums were grand structures. Swimming pools, an outdoor theater, a polo field and an Olympic Village that had 150 cottages for the male athletes were to be greatly admired. Nazi banners covered the Olympic complex. These games were the first to be filmed. Somerville could see some of the events in the news reels in movie theaters. The debut of the torch relay took place in the 1936 Olympics.

White supremacy was promoted openly. Hitler did not anticipate the role Jesse Owens would play in this competition. The games were underway. Jesse won four Gold Medals: the 100 meter dash, the long jump (an Olympic record), the 200 meter sprint around a turn (a world record), and part of the team for the 400 meter relay.

It was infuriating to Hitler to have a black man win over his *superio*r *blue eyed, blond, white skinned German athletes.* He had no power over the minds of the 4,000 athletes representing 40 countries who witnessed with their own eyes that Jesse Owens from the United States of America was clearly the most outstanding athlete competing in Berlin.

Coach Billy and Priscilla were enthusiastic cheerleaders as they watched their friend Jesse win these medals for their country. When Priscilla's races came up Jesse joined Coach Billy in cheering her on to her victories. Her first race was the 400- meter. Blessed with a quick start out of the blocks she easily won her first Gold Medal. Her second Gold was won as she was the fourth runner in the 400-meter relay. Between Jesse and Priscilla they were bringing six Gold Medals home to the U.S.

Chapter 24

They looked immediately to the Veranda where Charles had been playing the piano during the wedding. He wasn't there. The music had stopped!! Something dark seemed to invade the celebration. What had happened? Where was Charles?

Everyone began to search for this special young man. It was unlike him to leave his piano and wander off. No one had seen him leave. They searched the house and the grounds.

Armond and Little Henry left Hoss and Hannah's wedding and were playing tennis. The Wedding got to be a bit too mushy for these young teenagers. They were asked if they had seen Charles. Armond said, "We saw him awhile ago walking with Perro, his dog. They were headed toward the river."

Instead of music, panic filled the air. Everyone ran toward the mighty Mississippi River bank hoping against hope that he would be found in time. When they got to the bank, they found Perro alone. He was moaning as though he had witnessed his Master's disappearance.

Rescue efforts were put into place immediately. The rolling waters of the Mississippi put fear in every heart. If he had fallen into the water, the current would surely have carried him down the River quickly. All the men, including Hoss, joined the Rescue Squad. The banks of the River were searched and the waters dragged for days afterward.

Joy turned into sorrow in an instant. Plans for the Honeymoon were postponed. It all changed when the music stopped!

Two long weeks later, news came that a body was found washed up on the bank close to Natchez, Mississippi. The Deriveauxs, accompanied by the Chandlers, went hurriedly to identify the body. It was indeed their sweet child. It was Charles. Some would say that Charles was a sad life. But not his family. He was, indeed, a savant. He did not have normal communication skills. But he was God's child, made in God's image. Oh, and he was musically gifted and was a blessing to many people who had the privilege of hearing him play. The last thing he did in his life on this earth was to provide the music for this beautiful Wedding. Everyone there had the joy of feeling his music in their souls. Then the music stopped. Special grace from God had transported Charles into His Celestial Heaven where amazing music never stops. Charles was whole and holy in the presence of Almighty God.

His family grieved over his absence but rejoiced in knowing that he was free to worship God without being verbally challenged.

Fortunately, they had taped his music on many occasions and would never really be without his music.

Plans were made for Charles' Memorial Service. Many eulogies were shared. These were a comfort to Phillipe and Arienne and their children.

The most touching thing spoken that day was when Phillipe stood before the gathering of friends and family and shared his heart.

He said, "I confess my disappointment in being told that my Son was not 'normal'. I felt that I was being punished for something I had done and maybe something I had not done. Over the years, I came to see that Charles was indeed a special gift to our family. He was a teacher to me on many levels. Perhaps the most important thing he taught me was patience. I was awake during most of the past few nights with many hours to ask myself, "What is the true meaning of life." "Is it a brilliant mind, great physical strength or to obtain power through great wealth?" I concluded that this is Man's thinking, not God's. My son, Charles, could not measure up if that is what life is only about. God knew even before Charles was conceived that he was going to be special. I believe with all my heart that Charles is with God. Now to believe that, I must believe that God is Who He says He is. In the stillness and darkness of the night, the Light finally broke through to me. Many of the teachings from the Bible that Ephraim Chandler has shared with me over the past years came back to my mind. I had been blessed with health, wealth, a wonderful family and so much more. But if I was so intelligent that I could not accept by faith, what I couldn't prove in a test tube, I was of all men, the most ignorant. Last night, I bowed before God and confessed my sins to Him and asked Him to come into my lost life and save my soul. And He did just that!! So you see it was really Charles who finally got through my thick head and hardened heart. I know now that I will see Charles again. I will hear music like I have never heard before."

Everything seemed to go full circle. The joyous Wedding celebration where the music stopped; grief and sorrow invaded Somerville; joy was restored with the salvation of this dear man; and the sound of music returned.

Chapter 25

The news of Charles Deriveaux's tragic death was in every newspaper in Mississippi.

Leigh Ann had tried hard to keep her thoughts free of the past. It was too painful to think that she was separated from her precious little boy, Jean Luc. She had never questioned the reality that it was best for him to be raised by the Deriveauxs. After all, they could give him every material thing that he could ever need. She knew that they would love him as much as any of their own children.

Arienne had been faithful to her promise to send pictures of Jean Luc regularly.

Leigh Ann went to the Morgue as soon as she heard about the drowning. She knew the Deriveauxs would be there within hours of getting the news. She parked a safe distance from the Funeral Home. After a long wait, she saw two Cadillacs drive up. Her heart was racing! "Who will be getting out?" she asked herself. Philippe was the first and went around opening the door for his wife. Stepping out of the back was Edmond. She hadn't seen him in such a long time. He was still as handsome as ever. Old feelings surged through her heart. Tears ran down her cheeks as she remembered the young man she loved enough to give her virginity to him. Then there was the pain that followed as she thought of how she was just another trophy he desired for a brief time and then so easily tossed aside.

"Why, why was I so easily deceived by his debonair French charm? Why is he going on with his life without having to take responsibility for the suffering I've gone through? I hate him!! I wish he was the dead son instead of Charles. Dear God, I have always trusted You. Edmond has never believed in You. Is it fair that he is the one who seems to not even bear any part of this pain?

Oh, how I need to know that one day there will be answers that make sense so that I can have this burden lifted from my heart." Deep sobs shook her body as she released years of stored up pain.

Leigh Ann was not emotionally able to go to Arienne and express her condolences. She started her engine and returned to her home. Her mother was sitting on the porch when she arrived. It was obvious that her daughter was very upset.

"Leigh Ann, honey, whatever is wrong with you?"

"Nothing, Mama, I was just thinking about that poor young man who drowned. I don't know why it's upsetting me like this. But don't you worry. I'll just go in and wash my face and spend a little time by myself," said Leigh Ann.

After getting composed, Leigh Ann decided to write Arienne a note. She needed to tell her how sorry she was for her loss. Each one of them had experienced the pain of losing a child. Arienne had gone through this heartache when Vivian died and now with the death of Charles. Leigh

Ann's son was not dead physically, but the separation was like a death to her.

"Dear Mrs. Deriveaux,

I hesitated to write this note, but finally felt a deep need to do so.

I didn't know Charles except for my brief visit to your home several years ago. I did have the joy of hearing his beautiful music gracing your home. I will treasure that memory.

My heart broke for you when I heard that they had identified the body that washed up on our Natchez bank. It was Charles Deriveaux. It had to be your son as there are no other Deriveauxs that I know in Mississippi. I even went to the Funeral Home in the hope that I would see you. I stayed at a good distance, having no desire to make you uncomfortable. I simply needed to see you. You have always been gracious to me in the past. I am thankful to you for not completely shutting me out of my son's life. I know that I can not be there for him physically but you have blessed me with many pictures. He will forever be in my heart if not in my arms.

I pray every day that God will bless you and my child immeasurably.

Leigh Ann slipped into the room, unnoticed, where the family had left their personal things. She put the note in a pocket and left quickly.

The Deriveauxs returned to Somerville that same day. The hearse followed them with the body of Charles. Family and friends awaited their arrival at Somerville Funeral Home. Arrangements had already been put into place as to Visitation the next night and the Memorial Service the day after. Everyone was exhausted and made their way to the Deriveaux home. The kitchen was filled with casseroles, meats, vegetables and desserts. All of Somerville could have shared in the bounty. The only thing missing were some hearty appetites. Tonight was for rest. Tomorrow would require physical nourishment to get them through the next days.

After Arienne had retired to her bedroom, she changed into her gown. As she took her jacket off, she felt something in her pocket. There she found the note from Leigh Ann. As she read the words and felt the pain, the emotions lost control. She found herself talking out loud, as though somehow her words would penetrate space and comfort Leigh Ann.

"She was there and didn't feel that she could make her presence known to me. I loved this precious child and grieved when circumstances were such that she had no other choice but to give up her beautiful little boy to us. We have lost our son. We know he is with the Lord, and that is such a comfort. Leigh Ann's son is alive and well, living in the same state, and she can't see his first steps or his first tooth. She hasn't been able to pick him up when he falls, and hold him and wipe his tears and assure him that he will be alright. Her separation from her child will be a continuing heartbreaking experience. After I get through the Service for Charles, I will make plans to take Jean Luc to see his birth Mother. We will find a way for her to be a part of his life."

Then she climbed into her bed. The fresh crisp Battenberg sheets seemed to wrap around her tired body inviting her to relax and welcome the needed sleep.

Philippe was not able to relax enough to join Arienne. He got a glass of Chardonnay and made his way to the Music Room where Charles had spent much of his life playing the piano. He sat in the oversized leather chair with his feet on the matching ottoman. It seemed he could hear the music. In reality, the room was eerily quiet. Philippe found himself talking out loud just like Arienne had done.

"Why? Why? God, I don't understand why you would allow this horrible thing to happen to an innocent young man! I can't even fathom why you would have cursed him with that dreadful life of a Savant! I have asked many times, 'Was it because of something I did? I know I resisted any idea that I needed you to give my life meaning. I thought I had everything, wealth, health, power, and an amazing family. What did I need from you? But when my beautiful Vivien died tragically, I was awakened to the truth that I could not protect my family from bad choices and ultimate tragedies. I found myself seeking You with all my heart and you were there for me. But Lord, in order to live for You, must I give up two of my children? How many more will You take from me?" Manifold emotions surfaced, anger, frustration, guilt, and shame for questioning God gave way to tears. This strong man broke down and sobbed for such a long time. God then seemed to wipe away his tears and left His peace. God, for Charles's sake, let music fill Philippe's soul. He then sat his glass down and curled up in the chair and fell into an undisturbed night's sleep.

After a night's rest, everyone made their way to the dining room. Henry and Eliza had arrived earlier than usual to make sure everything was ready for the Deriveaux busy day.

Delightful smells traveled from the kitchen throughout the downstairs. Eliza had made her mouthwatering cinnamon rolls. The hazelnut cream coffee was an invitation to everyone to get downstairs as soon as possible. She, also, had scramble eggs, country ham and little homemade biscuits with butter and strawberry jam.

When they got to the table, Eliza took charge saying, "Now I'm gonna tell you rat up front, I'm not gonna hear of anybody saying they ain't hongry. Now, I knows you done been through a hard time. But that's when you gotta fill up yore stomicks with some solid food so's you can git through this day. Now, I done cooked for an hour, and I very well spect to see yo plates full when you start and empty when you leave."

Each family member got in lock step with Sargent Eliza and did it with a smile on their faces. One thing they knew was that Eliza did not say anything that she didn't mean. Plates were clean enough to almost put back in the cabinets. But, of course, they were carefully washed and dried.

All the family finished getting themselves ready for the day. Their first stop was at the Funeral Home to make sure that all the details had been worked out for the Visitation. The Funeral Home was not large enough to accommodate the number of people who would be coming to pay their respects. They would take the casket and flowers to the First Baptist Church.

The family went to the Florist to choose the Casket Spray. Since Charles was like an Angel to his family, they chose white to be the dominate theme. White roses and white gladiolas tied together with wide white satin ribbon covered the top of the mahogany casket. Brass handles were a handsome contrast to the mahogany. In honor of Charles, a local artist painted the music and words to his favorite hymn on the satin ribbon. The hymn was *Amazing Grace.* That grace of God that saved an innocent soul like Charles Deriveaux!

Chapter 26

A cloud of sadness seemed to have settled on Somerville after the tragedy of Charles' death. Where was the music? Where was the laughter? Every family found themselves wanting to stay in their own homes holding their dear ones close to them. Reality soon set in. There was still work to be done. They had to remember that their lives were in God's Hands. After all, didn't He say that our days are numbered? He did not say that our days were to be wasted. So after a short time, everyone returned to their jobs.

What they didn't know was that they would soon know the pain of losing one of their favorite people again. Eliza had suffered with high blood pressure and diabetes for many years. She had been told many times that she must lose some of the excess weight on her body. The doctor had impressed her with the need to rest and try to avoid stress.

Since she was the best cook in Somerville, it was hard for her to prepare all the sumptuous meals for the Deriveauxs and not save some for herself. So the pounds seem to continue to cling to her body. The death of Charles, who she adored, hit her very hard. As she had to make sure all the family and friends were fed and cared for along with caring for her own family, she had no time to rest.

For several days, she experienced headaches but never told anyone. It seemed that she was feeling more fatigued than usual. But that was easily explained by realizing that was due to the extra work load.

Usually she slept very soundly, but that night she was very restless and unable to stay asleep. The morning came and she got up but things weren't right. She found that she was off balance, leaning to the left. She held on to furniture as she made her way to the bathroom. Looking in the mirror, she noticed her eyes seemed to have moved to the left. The left side of her face had drooped in a very obvious way. She called for Henry.

Henry hurried to the bathroom. When Eliza turned to him and tried to tell him what had happened, he noticed the slur in her speech.

"Eliza, Honey, what's de matter wit you? You ain't lookin' right? I's gotta call the doctor quick." Before he could make the call, Eliza collapsed. Henry screamed for "Big John" to come and help him get her to the bed.

"Mary, you call the Doctor and tell him we gonna git her to the Hospital. Please meet us there. Then call Mr. Deriveaux and tell him why we ain't gonna be showing up for work today."

"Sarah, git' yo Mama a warm robe to put on. We don't want her to git' no chill."

"Little Henry, I want you to start praying hard that Mama's gonna be alright. I know you got a straight line to God, and He's gonna hear you."

"James, you and Luke go out and git' the car cleaned out so's we can lay yo Mama on the back seat. Big John's gonna drive me and Mama. The rest of you come on to the Hospital in the truck."

Then he went back to Eliza. Her pulse was slow. He knelt on the side of the bed and cradled her head in his arms.

"Please, Lord, don't let my Eliza die. You know how much we all need her here wit us. Now I know she's ready anytime you say she needs to go. But, Lord, I don't know how I would make it through a day without my Eliza. She's more than just a wife; she's my heart and soul. We done been married forty-eight years now. I know that's a long time for most people, but a hundred years wouldn't be enough for me. And Lord, if she knows what's happenin' to her now, please don't let her be afraid. I'll be talking to you again real soon, but now I gotta git her to the Hospital."

Big John carried his Mother gently to the car and put her in the back seat with her head on a pillow. They rushed to the Hospital.

Dr. Marquette met them there. After examining her carefully, he confirmed that Eliza had a massive stroke. The prognosis was grim. He promised to do everything possible to save her life. But they had to know that Eliza was in God's Hands now.

The family huddled together and cried and prayed. Very shortly, the Deriveauxs, the Chandlers and the Middletons all gathered to comfort Eliza's family. Several hours passed with no word from the Doctor.

About five o'clock that afternoon, Dr. Marquette came out and said there was nothing that could be done to save Eliza.

"If you want to go in and say your good-byes, now is the time to do it. She is in a coma. No one really knows whether she can hear you on some level or not."

Each child went in separately to kiss their Mother and tell her how much they love her. Broken hearts spilled buckets of tears. It seemed that Big John was inconsolable.

Then Henry went in to tell his wife one more time how he treasured their love. "My sweet Eliza, I wish I could change places with you. Everyone depends on you and needs you so much. I don't know what we's gonna do wit out you. But I want you to know that I'm gonna do my dead level best to take care of our youngun's like you always have. And, Baby, I's gonna hang on to what you always told us, 'God's got a place prepared for us in His Heaven and we's gonna all be together again one day.' I'm gonna hang on to that promise. I'll see you again real soon. In between now and then, you gonna still be here with us in yo' spirit, cuz it's gonna be in my heart always. I love you with all my heart! And I'm gonna miss you like crazy!"

He kissed her gently, place her head on the pillow and went back to be with his children.

Family and friends all followed Charlotte Chandler's lead as they comforted each other with the 23rd Psalm.

"The Lord is my Shepherd,
I shall not want.
He makes me lie down in green pastures;
He leads me beside quiet waters.
He restores my soul;
He guides me in the paths of righteousness
For His name's sake.

Even though I walk through
The valley of the shadow of death,
I fear no evil; for Thou art with me;
Thy rod and Thy staff, they comfort me.
Thou dost prepare a table before me
In the presence of my enemies;
Thou hast anointed my head with oil;
My cup overflows.
Surely goodness and loving kindness
Will follow me all the days of my life,
And I will dwell in the house
Of the Lord forever."

Dr. Marquette came out just as they finished.

"Eliza has seen Jesus face to face as of just five minutes ago. I can only imagine the joy she experience when Jesus showed her Charles. He had a perfect mind and body and I'm quite sure he played some Heavenly music to welcome her to her Heavenly home."

Somehow those words following scripture turned their sorrow into joy. Oh, they would miss Eliza each day that they remained on this earth. But the beautiful memories of this Proverbs 31 lady would always be cherished by those who knew and loved her.

This time, everyone gathered at the Jones' home where they could feel Eliza's presence. This house was a gift from friends who loved them after the evil force that came against them many years before and burned their home to the ground. Not a day passed that Eliza didn't remind her family of the way God took care of them during that frightening experience.

Ephraim took charge of making arrangements for the funeral service. As the word spread throughout the community, it seemed that everyone wanted to do something special for this dear family.

The Jones family attended a small church outside of town. There was no way that this Sanctuary could accommodate hundreds of mourners. Henry agreed that it would be better to let Ephraim arrange to use the First Baptist Church Sanctuary.

The viewing would be at the Somerville Funeral Home. All expenses were Philippe and Arienne's gift to their devoted and loyal employees. Hundreds of people came to the Visitation to speak to the family and view the body.

Everyone agreed that Eliza's Service was the most spiritually moving time they had ever experience. James wanted to play his Mother's favorite hymns on his guitar. He played "I won't have to cross Jordan alone" and "Beulah Land". Then little Henry, as he was always called, did the family eulogy. He was short in stature but powerful in the pulpit. He preached a sermon about this amazing servant of God, his Mother. There were a lot of "Amens" heard in the First Baptist Church that day.

Each child placed a red rose on Eliza's casket. Then Henry rose and went over to touch and kiss the casket that held his precious wife. Everyone heard him say, "Soon and very soon, I'll be comin' to meet you there. And there ain't gonna be no more separation for us ever again."

Nothing would ever be quite the same again in Somerville. Maybe it was because the heart and soul of this community left so suddenly. Oh, how they would miss Eliza Jones!

Chapter 27

Philippe's reminiscing came to an abrupt halt when he looked up and saw Ephraim Chandler standing over him.

"Philippe, it looked as though you were in some sort of trance."

"What time is it?" asked Philippe.

"Why, it's late afternoon," answered Ephraim. "How long have you been here? I thought you and Arienne were coming to our house for dinner."

"Forgive me. I have been awake all night. Eliza fixed me some breakfast and I suppose I slipped back in my thoughts of the past. It seems that I have recalled a lifetime of memories. The news of Pearl Harbor caused me to reflect on how uncertain life can be. We don't know what this day will bring. How precious is every minute we have with our loved ones! I feel as though strength has been drained from my body. Listen to me! I am rattling on like a magpie! I have never sensed such a need for family and friends to gather as one and confront this terror head on."

Ephraim put his arms around his friend and said, "My Brother, we will not give in to fear. When we all stand together knowing that God is all powerful and has promised to protect us and provide for us, how can we ever be less than conquerors? This attack is a terrorist move to destroy freedom loving people. Our country is not the only one suffering. Out of this mayhem, God will show Himself strong through His people, and we will triumph over this evil force."

"Now is the time for us to gather together and ask God to show us what we can do as we line up with His sovereign will." The two friends embraced and Ephraim left.

Arienne came downstairs looking for her husband. Finding him on the veranda, she asked, "What is it? Is something wrong?" He replied, "No, my Darling, I am fine. I just sat down to think about all the chaos around us last evening. My mind went back to France and our decision to come to America to give our children a better life. I discovered truths that will forever change my way of thinking. Circumstances did not transpire as I had planned. God had a different plan. We have grieved over the loss of two of our precious children. We have felt the pain of our friends who have suffered the same such losses. If we stop and dwell on these trials, we would be utterly helpless to go on. Then my thoughts turned to the realization that we had so many more blessings than pain. God brought you out of the clutches of literal death and gave you new life in Jesus Christ. All but one of our other children saw the change in your life and chose to follow your example and give their lives to Jesus. The most stubborn heart was mine. I fought the idea that I needed to die to myself in order to have eternal life with God in Heaven. However, with your Godly witness and the mentoring of Ephraim Chandler, even I said, "Yes" to God and exchanged my old stubborn life in for new life in Christ. So, you see, as I have reflected on the past years, I have concluded that the Deriveaux's were brought from Paris to Somerville in order that God might convict and convince us of our need for Him. Having said all of that, I promised Him and now I will promise you, I will spend the rest of my life in God's army, serving him with the same diligence that our family members, friends and neighbors are serving in this horror called World War II."

It was not too long before news began to break as to how the United States and her allies would respond. Great Britain and Russia aligned themselves with America.

The enemies were Germany, Japan and Italy. The battles would be fought on European soil. Now, there was a great need to prepare our military for World War II.

Young men from across the country were eager to volunteer for the Army (plus WAACS), Air Force and Navy (plus WAVES). There was a need for doctors and nurses to surrender to this call. Because so many men enlisted, it left businesses with few employees. Most women had been raised to be homemakers. However, the war required plants producing ammunition and materiel for the forces. Women rose up to meet this need by working along side men in the munitions plants.

Life as they had known it in the past was forever changed. No one wanted to be on the inside looking out. Everyone looked for the need they could meet.

It was not long before Hollywood organized celebrities to entertain the troops. Some movie stars wanted to be actively engaged in the war itself. They left their lucrative careers to be fighter pilots. Patriotism was at an all time high.

It was the worst of times! It was the best of times!

From Somerville's best, volunteers like the Chandler's son, Benjamin, Henry Jones' daughters, Mary and Sarah, Millicent's sons, William and Lawrence, and her daughter, Priscilla, rose quickly to the challenge of joining the thousands of their fellow Americans ready to do their part in protecting their country.

To everyone's surprise, the Deriveaux's son, Edmond put his ambitions to be in politics on hold, and volunteered for the Air Force. Edmond had never thought of anyone's needs except his own. He willingly gave up his father role to his parents when little Jean Luc was born. Edmond told his parents that he had what he described as a "clarion call" from God to join those who were sacrificing for a greater good. At no time in his life had he experienced the satisfaction that comes from selflessness. That was not a word in his dictionary.

That day came when the buses drove up to Main Street in Somerville to take many young men to Camp Shelby near Hattiesburg, Mississippi, for basic training in the Army. A few went in other directions. Edmond was sent to the Air Force Academy to prepare for Officer's training and for his pilot's license. Benjamin chose the Navy and was sent to Pensacola, Florida, for his training.

It seemed as though someone came through Somerville and rode off with their finest young men and women. Many tears were shed, hugs and kisses abounded, hands waved good-bye, and those remaining went to their homes to begin the adjustment process.

For those left at home, their job was to lift up their loved ones and the leaders of their country and its allies to the Lord God in diligent prayer. Faith in God was the common bond that drew them closer to each other than ever before. Each person felt the need to reach out and meet the needs of their friends and neighbors. Victory in this War would depend upon God's power and leadership. God raised up President Franklin D. Roosevelt, Prime Minister of England, Winston Churchill and Joseph Stalin of Russia, to join in an alliance to defeat Adolph Hitler's insane effort to destroy the free world.

Printed in the United States
By Bookmasters